"What is a person's age?

Is it the body's clock,
ever ticking, ticking?
Or is it something else,
nebulous, indefinable?

How, then, do we
characterize ourselves?
Chronologically, or by
how we engage life?"

--- James Fulcher

TEASER

A Love Story
That Spans
The Generations

JAMES FULCHER

Also by James Fulcher:
Time-Shift: In A Future World
Clone One, Prototype 13

With gratitude to my author friends for their invaluable help and gracious patience.

"Teaser", Second Edition.

ISBN: 978-1451550764.

Dedicated to Sandi, my muse

ONE

Early Spring, 1999

The old motorcycle just wouldn't start. It would sputter and even pretend to idle for a brief moment, but it wouldn't take any throttle. Every time the teen stood on the kick-starter and then lunged downward with all his might, it sent ripples of agony through his leg and ankle, and the big V-twin seemed to just chuckle at him. It was as if she were saying, "Ha ha, you twit of a boy; it'll take a real man to stroke me."

He had tried adjusting the rusted and pitted choke lever but had only succeeded in creating smelly fumes of gasoline. The noxious odor permeated the air and reminded him of the smells at the Johnson Refinery where his father had been working for the boy's entire life.

A noise startled him and he quickly scanned the area but thankfully it was only a squirrel scurrying along with something in its mouth. He didn't want anyone to see his inability to start the obstinate relic. But he didn't think of it as a relic even though she had seen her better days long before he was even born. To him she was the greatest possession he could even imagine. She was beautiful to his naïve eyes and he didn't see any of the dents, rust, or faded paint. He saw instead a glorious machine of unimaginable power, a flight of fancy to far-away places and marvelous adventures awaiting his lusting soul.

If only she would consent to his demand to start and run for him. He knew she could run because he had ridden her home and carefully hidden her behind the shed. But it had been the old man who had coaxed the hesitant beast into life, and now it wouldn't respond. Maybe he had been right, that only someone wise in the ways of women could elicit the needed response. And even though Rocky had just last month achieved what he believed to be the mature and grown-up age of 17, he was still just a boy when it came to the mysteries of the opposite but ever so desirable other sex. And now the lady between his legs wasn't planning to respond to him with anything more than a tease. *Please start,* he thought. *I don't know how to make you happy, but I'm trying. Please trust me and start.*

Finally, exhausted and sore, Rocky laid his body with its acutely aching leg and ankle onto the ground next to the stubborn machine. The snow had disappeared from his yard a few weeks before and a pleasant early April breeze cooled him through his sweat soaked shirt. The browned winter grass rubbed roughly but he only thought of how wonderful it felt to just lay down for a bit.

He loved the secluded and unkempt little spot in his back yard. It was his favorite place and it was there that he spent many hours lost in his colorful imagination.

He was hidden from the house by the garage back wall and hidden from the nearest neighbors by thick stands of oak and pine trees with an abundance of undergrowth that hadn't been cut back for many years, except for one secret pathway that he had kept passable since he was a boy. The front door to the garage hadn't been closed for such a long time that it would no longer pivot on its hinges, and the walk-through door in the garage's back wall was quite wide and provided easy access for him and his motorcycle. The garage itself was set back from the house a good twenty feet which added to the solitude of his private retreat. But even so he dare not start the engine while anyone was in the house; the machine may have been old, but she hadn't lost any of her deep, throaty rumble.

Innocently, or perhaps carelessly, he looked up at the blue sky with just a hint of clouds and almost immediately fell into his imaginary dream world of adventure and travel. As long as he could remember this wonderful world of pleasure or pain had called to him at every opportune moment, and frequently at inopportune moments as well. In his real life world he needed an escape and his vivid imagination poised ever ready to jump to his rescue. His imaginary and private world of wonderment brought many hours of pleasure and escape. But there were also many times when it overpowered him at poorly chosen moments, after which his inattention to the task at hand would cost him a painful price when he had to finally face the consequences. And if the consequences involved his father, the pain was sometimes substantial.

On that Wednesday Rocky's father was working the dayshift at the refinery and his mother was off to her weekly ladies bible study and potluck down at the church. He had plenty of time to fuss over his new acquisition, but once he laid down and let his imagination start to run loose the minutes and hours could easily slip away and before he knew it his mother would be home. Unfortunately, he had never been very good at knowing when his loss of reality would get him into trouble.

Lying and resting on the ground, his imagination instantly took flight. *I remember my first ride on you, my lady. I remember every detail even though I was only the passenger. That was the most special day I'd ever had. The best thrill of my life. Now please start for me. Then we can have thrills together. You even helped give me my nickname. Do you remember? You're the reason I'm Rocky now.* He frequently thought about that day long ago, and how he had tenaciously held onto his nickname even when everyone was so used to calling him Tom. Now, only his mother called him Tom, and even then only when she was upset about something.

But his daydreams didn't stay in the past very long. Within moments he imagined himself riding his newfound motorcycle down a long 2-lane country highway. He glanced in the rear view mirror mounted on the left handlebar and saw everything in his world disappearing away behind him. With the wind in his hair and the rumble of the mighty engine between his legs, setting his soul on fire, the imaginary Rocky wasn't tired or aching or frustrated. He was just simply free.

------- <<>> -------

The old man, Clint Larkins, awoke that morning with a deep sadness that seemed to grip every cell of his pain wracked body. He had been dreading this day for a decade now, although at times even recently it had seemed only a distant possibility rather than something that pressed him harder every day.

The early morning sun was shining though the many cracks and holes in his makeshift shanty. He had removed the tarp that kept them covered during the winter just a few days before. The pressure in his bladder felt relentless and impatient. His deep sadness would have kept him wrapped in his blankets for hours longer, but the pressure and fullness in his gut were more powerful than his mental state. And it didn't matter that he might only pee a little bit anyway. He had long ago made peace with the fact that his swollen prostate would only relent for a dribble at a time.

Slowly he worked his way to a standing position and made his way outside into the woods he so loved. The Shenandoah Valley had been mostly all forested when he was a boy, with a patchwork of cleared areas belonging to family farms. Then, over the years, more trees had been cleared or logged, more homes built, and the towns had generally increased in size. He wasn't interested in living a mountain man's life, or that of a trapper or hunter, but nevertheless he loved the woods and had always lived close to or in wooded areas.

He knew that as he moved around during the morning his body would regain a tad of the flexibility it had once known, but his profound sadness seemed to want to rob him of even that relief. He couldn't hold his release long enough and had to stop just a few feet past the entryway and yank down his zipper just before he wet himself. And, as he had known, only a dribble came out. *Wouldn't have mattered,* he thought, *if I'd just wet myself. Couldn't have made me any sadder than I already am. Seems ironic, somehow.*

It would be a couple of hours before he'd have the flexibility and strength to kick-start his old motorcycle to life. And what a magnificent machine she had been back in her day. He may have owned the machine, but her spirit was owned by no one. But all of that was in the past, and today she was going to leave him forever.

The sadness of it brought tears to his eyes when he turned and gazed upon her aged but so familiar beauty. *You're so like a woman, aren't you old girl? So cold yet so warm, so selfish yet so giving, and always a teaser.* He walked to her and gently touched the worn leather saddle while tears ran down his face and spattered on his love. Then angrily he said to the machine, "I'll divorce you. That's what I'll do. I'll divorce you and then be done with you." He turned away with tears still wetting his cheeks.

Divorce? I could never divorce you, my love. Never. His mind as sharp as ever, he muttered, "Curious, it is," as he continued to dwell on the meaning of it all. He had never left a woman, but his one and only bride had left him oh so many years before. And she hadn't even said goodbye. "At least I'll say goodbye to you, soon," he gently and sadly said to his motorcycle. "But I won't just up and abandon you like Meredith did to me," he added as he vividly remembered.

TWO

Earlier that same morning the clock-radio had come to life with its usual loud music. The volume was especially loud because its owner had known the night before that he could get away with it on that particular morning. Rocky rolled over but didn't open his eyes. There would be time enough to do that in a few minutes, but he wanted to stay in bed and listen to the song that was playing. The mornings were still cold even though the days were warming nicely, and the bed covers felt wonderful. Hazily, half-awake, he wondered why he had set the clock-radio for a day when there was no school.

Then with a jump that was so sudden it surprised even himself, he was sitting straight upright in bed. He had just remembered what day it was, and his instant excitement had brought him to being fully awake and alert. It was to be the greatest day of his entire life and he wasn't going to waste a moment of it lying in bed. So off to the bathroom he rushed to relieve himself. Then within minutes he was dressed and ready for the day, except for one vitally important detail. He went to the secret hiding place in the back of his closet and retrieved the $182 he had been saving. It was a lot of money, more than he had ever had before, but he was anxious to part with it on that lovely morning.

"Mom!" he yelled even before he was out of his bedroom. "Mom! Where are you?"

------- <<>> -------

Wilma Powlison didn't like yelling in her house. She didn't even like loud conversation. And she certainly didn't like Rocky's loud music, although she tried to tolerate it because he was after all a teenager. She did everything she possibly could to keep the house quiet and peaceful, never playing music just for herself, never turning the TV loud, and never leaving the TV on when it wasn't being watched. When her husband wasn't home it was always peaceful. Except, that was, when her son yelled at her from across the house.

Instead of her usual reaction, on that particular morning Mrs. Powlison wasn't going to punish Rocky for yelling in the house. It was her bible study and potluck day, and she knew it would be a sin to get angry before going to church later in the morning. She loved the Wednesday get-togethers and wasn't going to do anything sinful that might make the Father not welcome her into His church. So she waited for Rocky to come and find her in the kitchen where she was baking some of her famous apple tarts for the ladies at the potluck. When he appeared she simply said, "Good morning, dear. You know we don't yell in the house when your father isn't home."

"Sorry, Mom. Is breakfast ready?" he asked, obviously very excited about something.

"Not yet, it's not time yet. Why are you so early this morning, Rocky? Did you forget there's no school today?"

She didn't realize it, but he was in trouble with that question, as he hadn't considered how to explain his sudden eagerness to get going. Usually she had to tell him several times to go or he'd be late for school, and when school was out like it was that day for a teacher planning session he always slept in. She would pamper him on those days, and fix his breakfast later in the morning, whenever he wanted it. *After all, he's a good boy and always does his homework, and soon enough he'll be in the working world where no one will be pampering him.*

Her question startled Rocky, who wasn't always very quick to figure out what to say when he needed to get out of a situation, and that lack of being able to lie on cue frequently got him into a painful confrontation with his father. He didn't like to lie, especially to his mom, and he wasn't very good at it, but sometimes it couldn't be avoided. He knew he had to tread carefully.

Then, in a flash of unexpected inspiration, he blurted out, "I'm going up to Old Maid's Creek today and I want to get a good start." She didn't suspect anything because he always enjoyed hiking up there, and his excitement that morning was obvious.

"Well, you be careful up there, dear. The spring runoff's strong this time. You stay out of that creek, you hear?" she asked as his breakfast eggs hit the skillet.

"Sure Mom," he replied, relieved that there weren't any glitches popping into his plans for the day.

The moment he finished eating he gave his mom a quick hug and asked her to save him some apple tarts then he was gone. She always melted when he gave her a hug, even the little quick ones that were the best she ever got since he had become a teen. *Even a quick hug from my son is ever so much better than nothing at all, and some of my friends don't even get that much from their children. What a perfect day I'm having; my husband is off at work, I have bible study, a potluck, and now a hug from my son!* She didn't know why Rocky would sometimes do it, and usually it was completely unexpected. But it always filled her heart with love and her eyes with tears.

------- <<>> -------

The bicycle sat unused in the garage, leaning against the boxes next to the wall. Rocky wouldn't be needing it that day. Sometimes he still rode it, but more often he just walked. He liked walking with the forest close by, even though there were more and more houses along the way now. And he especially liked the solitude. His school and the town were less than half an hour's walk, and the school bus was available if the weather was bad. But walking was a joy, and his imagination would usually soar along far ahead of him. Many times his thoughts involved girls in his school, and he wished he had a girl friend. Then he wouldn't be walking by himself, he always imagined. But those were wishes only, and the reality was that dating wasn't easy with an unreliable father to act as chauffeur. So he hadn't made much of an effort to foster any such relationships. It didn't help his self-confidence any, either, that his father frequently teased him about not having a girl friend, sometimes calling him a "gay-boy". But gay he certainly wasn't, and the nice enough looking, blond, blue-eyed young man that he was, with a good build from doing part-time farm work, attracted a bit of interest from the girls. Especially as they got to know him and saw that he had a pleasant manner and wasn't prone to showing off around them. He knew that once he had his own transportation he could find a girl to date. But until then he couldn't trust having his father involved in his dating life, and borrowing the family car just wasn't in the cards. And he certainly wouldn't want his mother to drive him and a girl, so he just didn't really date.

That day, though, was completely different. He seemed to be gliding along on a cushion of air, floating effortlessly and beautifully, feeling the warmth of the morning sun, and loving life. He didn't even notice the forest or the roadway, and was barely aware of the occasional car that went by forcing him to walk to the side for a bit. His imaginary adventures weren't filled with girls at all; instead it was something new and exciting, wonderful and magical. It was going to be the biggest and best day there had ever been. He reached yet again into his pocket to check for the $182. He had checked the same pocket so many times already that morning and was wondering why he felt he had to do it yet again, but again he did it anyway. It had taken him a long time to save $182, and now he could barely wait to get rid of it.

------- <<>> -------

Clint's sadness was profound. The old man couldn't bear thinking about selling his beloved motorcycle later that day, and then his thoughts were betraying him with even more sadness, as he began thinking about his Meredith. He had such fond and plentiful memories of her, but every fond memory also had the underlying sadness and depression that had plagued him since she disappeared out of his life so unexpectedly. But there she was, fresh in his mind, and he knew once she was in there she wouldn't be leaving quickly. Thoughts of his beloved motorcycle faded away until all he could think about was Meredith, way back when he first knew her.

Those had been such happy times, back 53 years when he had fallen in love with the girl that would become the prom queen. His then boyish love contradicted his fear, because after all he didn't really have a chance with someone so beautiful and desirable. Meredith was the beauty of his high school and all the handsome young men chased after her. He watched her attentively and knew she loved all the attention and fuss they made over her. She was quite the tease, but never in a malicious way. It's no wonder he had seen a glimmer in her, a glimmer of something so fine and pure that he just knew there was a real down-to-earth person under the beauty queen façade. After all, he had always been very astute about human nature, even from an early age. And that astuteness would be his ally in the greatest task of his young life.

He saw that Meredith seemed wise in the ways of dealing with boys, and their rural high school outside of Roanoke, VA must have presented a marvelous opportunity for her since she was immediately the most lovely and desirable girl in the entire school.

Her straight blond hair, beautiful blue/green eyes, and overall beauty always caught everyone's attention, but those outer attributes didn't do justice to her inner self. She was kind and compassionate even at her young age, very bright, and blessed with a quiet determination that only her very best friends ever saw clearly. But Clint sensed it, and combined with her looks she was completely irresistible to him.

So he set about creating a plan to win her over. A task worthy of the most clever of lovers, it would be, although he wasn't quite sure what "lover" actually meant. He knew it would take a considerable time because Meredith wasn't likely to even notice a plain fellow such as himself. Even in the classes they shared there were always jocks and other popular boys trying to get to her. But most importantly, he knew if he didn't try for her then he would feel a failure for the rest of his life, and with that thought he was compelled to do or die. What he didn't know, and never could have guessed, is that the first love of his life, right there in his high school, would bring to him the final love of his life that the old man was preparing to part with on that very day.

His fledgling grand plan was grounded on his feeling that Meredith was a sensible, down-home kind of girl under her beauty and boy-magnet exterior. He just had to set it up so they could get to know each other and he was sure she would like him, although that sureness was quite arrogant based on his history, or rather non-history, with girls. And so his plan was born and nurtured, and the arrogance of foolish youth lived on in the complete security of his full denial of reality. The grand plan would have successive phases, he decided, which meant that he didn't have to figure it out completely in advance. That was indeed very good, because at that point he didn't have a clue as to what the more advanced phases might be. But he knew one thing for certain – he didn't stand a chance against the jocks and popular boys if he tried to compete with them out in the open. So, sneaky became his watchword. But not sneaky in a bad way, just sneaky so he could implement Phase 1 of his plan without it being obvious to anyone, most especially to Meredith herself.

The grand plan would begin with the obvious. He had to meet the goddess face-to-face. That would be Phase 1. Since they shared several classes he thought that could certainly be arranged. But there was a rather significant problem, one not so easy to deal with as simply arranging to meet. The problem had to do with his nervousness around girls. One reason he had never asked a girl on a date was because he always got queasy in his stomach whenever he was close to a cute girl, and he was afraid of vomiting on someone if he tried to ask her out. Meredith was not in any way just a 'cute girl,' she was the epitome of cute girls. Throwing-up had moved from merely a vague possibility to something more akin to an absolute. So the meeting had to be done in a very simple, casual way with lots of people around to keep him somewhat distracted.

He started praying every day that he would be calm when he met her. Calm and peaceful, calm and relaxed, calm and not queasy, calm and not embarrassed, calm and handsome, calm and manly, and of course just plain calm. He wasn't much of a church person, but he did have a firm belief in the Creator and the power of prayer. As if it were a miracle, just two days later opportunity played right into his not quite calm hands.

Meredith had accidentally forgotten some papers in the storage tray under her student's chair when she left history class that afternoon. He saw them even as she was getting up to leave after the bell rang, but he couldn't get his mouth to open so he could simply tell her. This actually worked to his advantage because he retrieved her papers then had time to talk to himself about being calm, relaxed and self-assured. He did this all the way to the cafeteria while following well behind her. She went directly to the serving line and he got in line with two other students between them.

"Meredith?" he croaked. His voice was so tight and constricted that fortunately she didn't hear his feeble attempt to speak. But now was his big chance to get this done while in a group and while no boys were busy hitting on her. So he cleared his throat, summoned even more courage, and tried again. "Meredith?" came out better this time and she turned and looked at him with an expression that was non-committal.

She recognized him and smiled and said, "Oh, hi. You're in my history class aren't you?"

"Yes," he said, not knowing where he was going to get the courage to continue. But then somehow he managed to say, "I'm Clint Larkins. You left these papers in class." He shoved the papers past the two students between them. She reached out her hand and was barely able to grasp them before he bolted and almost ran out of the cafeteria, leaving her with a puzzled look on her face. Boys usually took every opportunity to keep talking to her about any dumb thing they could think of, even if she didn't really want them to, and there was this strange boy running away from her. If Clint had been able to look back at her, he would have seen that his behavior had completely confused her.

For Clint's part, he didn't have time to notice her expression. He headed straight to the boys' room, which to everyone's good fortune was very close, and chucked in the toilet. After that he was too embarrassed to go back to the cafeteria so he just walked around until his next class started. Fortunately Meredith wasn't in that class so he wouldn't have to face her right away.

THREE

The bright spring morning was still young and the air crisp with the lingering nighttime chill from the recent winter, but Rocky, who usually noticed everything on his walks along the road to town, hadn't noticed any of it. The hustle and bustle in and around Johnson's Crossing on that Wednesday morning, like every other mid-week morning, consisted mostly of locals going to work and farmers coming and going. The surrounding farms were still predominately family owned, as they had been for generations. There weren't any tourist destinations close by the township, so there wasn't a lot of through traffic, which was just how the residents seemed to like it. The Town Council always turned down the occasional attempt to modernize or expand the business district.

But the general proximity to Roanoke had, in the previous few years, resulted in an influx of well-to-do families that were looking for a rural home environment within commuting distance, even if it was a long commute. Land values had soared, at least in the opinions of the locals, and some of the farmers were selling parcels to outsiders for country estates. The population had never been very high in Johnson's Crossing so there were still large parcels with old-growth forests standing proudly; city people were also buying chunks of those forested parcels to build homes surrounded by trees, something they couldn't get in the city. Rocky's walk into town took him past several smallish farms, then past some expansive estate homes that had been built within the last few years. Those were interspersed amidst some remaining forested areas, which were his favorites along the walk.

Johnson's Crossing had always been a rural farm town, without significant industry or manufacturing. The main street, aptly named Main Street, was a series of shops and service businesses, many of them in former homes that had been converted into businesses over the years. Main Street also had a generous spattering of vacant lots and a few vacant buildings, and an occasional residence sandwiched between some of the businesses. There were a few other streets that together made up the business district, but to a city person it all had the appearance of a small, quaint old farm town. There were several places along Main Street where the forest came up right behind the buildings, which gave the whole town a certain character and feel. It was commonplace to see deer in town, and an occasional coyote.

Jeremiah Johnson, for whom the town had been named, was also the founder of the nearby Johnson Refinery, which had grown over the years to become the only large employer in town. The area had ample oil even though it was in smallish pockets that took a lot of drilling to find, and Mr. Johnson had built his refinery long ago to serve the oil wells that were scattered in a seemingly haphazard way around the area.   Eventually he sold out to a larger regional oil company but he wanted to insure his legacy so he insisted they not change the refinery's name.   One thing that did change, though, was that the larger oil company was unionized so they had upgraded the salaries and benefits at their newly acquired facility.   Landing a job there was considered quite a plum even though it could also be a dangerous place to work.   No other employer in town offered the pay and benefits available at the refinery, and a breadwinner's job there could spell the difference between near poverty for his or her family and the ability to have a comfortable life.

With the influx of well-to-do families from Roanoke, Johnson's Crossing was slowly being forced into becoming more urban, but for now it still got along fine as a small rural farm town.   With television and radio, the local young people were feeling the call and enticements of a faster lifestyle in the city, and many were leaving as soon as they finished high school.   But it was different for Rocky, even though he had spent his entire young life there.   The call he heard was not from the city, but rather from the open road.

Rocky wasn't noticing the forest or much of anything that morning as he walked along toward town. He usually heard every bird, every squirrel, and every other sound the forest made.   He usually noticed the houses along the way, always wondering about the people that had built those large homes over the last few years. That day, his only thoughts were about the old man and the motorcycle.

His $182 had just been put back in his pocket for the umpteenth time, when he wondered why the old man wanted exactly that amount.

"182 dollars. No more. No less," Clint had told Rocky a couple of months ago when he had inquired about purchasing the motorcycle.

He mused on that one for a bit, but then his thoughts went way, way back. He couldn't remember the first time he met Clint, but then again he couldn't remember ever not knowing him, either. Whenever his mom took him to town she always did some shopping at Gold's Pharmacy where Clint worked as the head pharmacist. The routine always started off in the same way …

"Uncle Clint!" he would holler as soon as he got to the door, Rocky recalled fondly.

"Tom, you mind your manners. His name is Mr. Larkins," was always his mother's immediate reproach to her son. He hadn't earned his nickname yet in those younger days.

Then Clint would smile and tell him, "I'm Uncle Clint to you, my boy." His happiness to see Clint, who wasn't really his uncle at all, was then invariably reinforced with the offer of a piece of candy from the goody counter. Clint then always tried to spend a few moments with him even if the pharmacy counter was busy.

Rocky smiled to himself as he recalled those happy memories. Clint was always nice to him, and if time permitted sometimes they would even sit on the bench out in front of the pharmacy. His mom would sometimes join them when she had finished her shopping, and she and Clint always seemed happy to see each other.

He always pestered his mom to let him go with Uncle Clint for a motorcycle ride, and she always said no. Until, that is, his seventh birthday. That day must have been a slow one for Clint, Rocky recalled, because both the man and his mom were with him on the bench beside the pharmacy's front door. He proudly announced to Clint that it was his birthday and inquired what present might there be for him that day.

Feigning an upset, Wilma quickly chastised him. "Hush, child! Where are your manners? Don't you go asking Mr. Larkins for a present. It's not polite and you know it."

"Oh Wilma, let the boy ask. It isn't everyday a young man turns seven, after all. And Tom should be proud to be that age now. He can ask me for a present any time he wants." Then he turned to Tom and asked, "What will it be today, Tom? We just got in some new toys. I'll bet there's something there you'll like. So what'll it be for you on this important birthday?"

Clint never seemed upset with Tom for asking for anything, although he would always say no if Tom's mom said he shouldn't have whatever it was. The boy's requests for a ride on the motorcycle were always denied by her, but candy or some sort of trinket or toy that the pharmacy stocked on its shelves was practically always rewarded. But more than that, he always felt like Uncle Clint genuinely enjoyed seeing him, and he fondly remembered their times together on the bench out front.

Emboldened by Clint's comment to his mom, Tom took a chance. "I'd like a ride on your motorcycle." He saw Clint looking over at his mom, and he knew she would say no like she always did. He started to get up and go look at the new toys in the store when she said something he thought he'd never hear.

"I guess it would be OK this one time." She then quickly added, "That is if Mr. Larkins has the time for it today. Otherwise, it's a new toy for you, Tom."

Rocky recalled that day vividly. He was so surprised at what his mother said that he couldn't open his mouth to say anything. He just sat there. Then he suddenly realized that it was now up to Uncle Clint whether or not he would get the best present ever. He instantly jumped into Clint's lap and threw his arms up around the man's neck and, with his face inches away from Uncle Clint's, looked him straight in the eyes and waited, still unable to utter a single word.

Clint had been watching Meredith intently since the day she had transferred into his 10th grade class from a big school in Atlanta. It's a wonder she hadn't felt his eyes so often burning into her. He didn't think about it very much, but when he did he supposed she was so used to being watched by boys that she didn't sense his intrusion as being that of just one individual. Every detail of her face and hair and body had become permanently etched into his very being. He knew every blouse, every skirt, every pair of pants, every pair of shoes, and every piece of jewelry that she ever wore to school. If she happened to wear something in a different combination he immediately memorized it.

His obsession with the elusive young woman was complete and all consuming. He knew her mannerisms, her speech patterns, and how she delivered her flirtatious and teasing comments to the other boys. Fortunately his total obsession wasn't dangerous, except to himself when he couldn't concentrate on anything else. He felt very lustful toward his dream girl, but there was much more to it than just hormones in his groin, although there was plenty of that. He saw that the other boys all felt and acted lustful towards her, but he wanted Meredith for much more than that; he had sensed that she was quite a special person and he wanted the whole package. He was completely in love with her and wanted her as his girl friend so badly it hurt in his heart when he saw her frequently talking to other boys. She was so popular, and had so many boys to choose from, that any thoughts of ever having her were pure foolishness, yet his emotions and hormones overwhelmed him and obscured reality.

He could picture her clearly even with his eyes closed, a very useful ability that he took full advantage of when he went to bed every single night, no matter how late the hour or how tired he felt. He would think of her while lying in his bed and his young body always responded acutely to his thoughts, even on those occasions when his thoughts weren't erotic. He used so many tissues he became concerned that his mother would notice the ever dwindling supply, so he would go to the store and buy them himself to keep her from catching on and discovering what he was doing so much of. Then he always carefully flushed the evidence away in the morning.

He still remembered that first day he had seen Meredith in early December when she seemed to glide into his 10th grade homeroom and went right up to Mr. Davidson's desk, just like she wasn't afraid of him at all. He knew that everyone in the entire room watched her intently, and not just because she was the new kid coming into a school where most of the students had known each other their whole lives. Everyone watched Meredith simply because she was so lovely, so radiant, and so much the epitome of what every teen boy wanted to possess as his girlfriend. And she had an exotic look to her, something he couldn't put his finger on, but whatever it was it made her all the more enchanting and desirable.

The days went by, with Clint looking forward to every morning when he would see his dream girl again. Every day he watched her as she breezily went about the social process she had immediately undertaken when she had first appeared at his Cooper High School. It was so easy for her, so natural, that practically every boy in the school was drawn to her and she loved enticing them. With her beauty and the way she instinctively knew just how to tease and toy with the boys it was a wonder the other girls didn't get together and just do her in. Most of the girls never warmed up to Meredith, but they didn't seem to out and out hate her, which was a testament to her natural way with people. Meredith never teased or toyed with the girls, so there were a few that actually made friends with her. Those girls would defend her anytime there was a hint of nastiness or gossip, and they seemed to benefit from their friendship with the beauty as much as Meredith enjoyed having them as friends.

Clint's grand plan to win her over had progressed through Phase 1, which was to meet her so he could start saying "Hi" to her every morning in home room. So far it was the best he could do and he sometimes dwelled on the folly of his plan. *I'm no match for those jocks. There's no point in trying to move my plan along. They keep making plays for her and she loves their attention. Somehow she seems to keep all of them interested. But I don't think she accepts dates with them. How does she do it? And why doesn't she go out with them? I betcha if there was a contest for being able to string multiple boys along, she'd get the grand prize.* Watching the feeding frenzy made him very sad and depressed because he knew he wasn't as handsome as some of them, and if they were striking out then he wouldn't have a snowball's chance in wherever. But he did keep up with praying every day that his plan to win her over might somehow beat the odds and miraculously work.

Clint wasn't homely or anything, and might even be considered cute or good looking by a generous observer. But he wasn't a handsome jock. However, in his great good fortune, what he lacked in super looks and sports skills he made up for with astuteness and patience. Eventually he managed to summon the courage to formulate Phase 2 of his grand plan, then he started to plan his movements and activities to create opportunities to have brief interactions with Meredith. But he never asked her for anything and was careful to never overstay the briefness of the connections, even though his heart hurt every time he walked away from her. He didn't know if his plan would work, but it was at least different from what the other boys were trying. This also had the benefit of allowing him to get somewhat used to being close to her and exchanging a few words, so his acute nervousness had calmed down a good bit. Whenever he thought of taking his plan to the next level he would still get queasy and nauseous, sometimes quite so, but the brief encounters had become well tolerated and he had begun to extend the simple "Hi" to some longer exchanges about a teacher or class or some particular homework assignment.

To his amazement and great huge joy his hard work started to pay off as Meredith came to know him and she began to like him as a person and didn't just see in him a boy trying to get somewhere with her. She actually began to trust him and would even seek him out sometimes in the cafeteria or during study hall. Before long they had actually spent several study hall sessions sitting together working on various homework assignments. Phase 2 was nearing completion. He was simply beside himself with glee.

FOUR

"Please."

The tiny whisper had barely escaped through Tom's tightly constricted throat and mouth. But it was enough to loosen him up just a bit and he then said, "Please, Uncle Clint."

Tom hadn't moved. His arms were still around Clint's neck and he was looking straight into the man's eyes, which were only inches away. Now he just waited again. It seemed an eternity.

Then Clint hugged him and said, "Of course I'll take you for a ride. After all, what would a seventh birthday be like if it didn't include a motorcycle ride for my favorite boy Tom?"

The moment Clint released his hug, Tom jumped off his lap like a flash and raced around beside the pharmacy to the grassy area where Uncle Clint always parked his pride and joy. He stood beside the huge gleaming machine and couldn't stop himself from jumping up and down with excitement.

His mom came around the building and told him that Mr. Larkins would be there in a moment. She then told the boy, "Now you do exactly what Mr. Larkins tells you. Don't jump around on the back of the motorcycle. And hold onto Mr. Larkins with your arms around him the whole time." She kissed and hugged and asked him, "Do you understand?"

"Yes Mommy. I'll do what Uncle Clint says. Is he almost here?"

Just then Clint appeared and told him, "You stand there while I get her started up. Sometimes she teases me and won't start right away, so we have to wait until she's running. Then I'll get you onboard. Ok?"

"Ok!" was his quick reply. He then watched Clint getting the mighty machine ready, doing all of the settings and adjustments that he didn't understand. It culminated with Clint standing up on the starter lever and giving a mighty lunge downwards to start the engine. Nothing happened. Another mighty lunge, and this time the machine roared into exuberant life.

It was so sudden and loud that Tom jumped back and tripped over a large rock, falling completely down. But he wasn't hurt and jumped upright so fast that he tripped over the rock again. Clint and Wilma couldn't help but laugh out loud at his nervous and excited attempt to recover from his momentary clumsiness. "Got to watch those rocks," Clint told him. "They can get in the way of motorcycles, too. Now come here and I'll help you on. But don't touch anything unless I tell you to because some places will get real hot."

He scampered onto the rear seat with Clint's guidance and put his arms tightly around the man's waist and held on for dear life. He couldn't see directly in front to see where they were going, but he wasn't thinking of that at all because just getting a ride was going to be his greatest thrill.

"Don't you worry now, Wilma," Clint said. "He'll be just fine and we'll be back in a little while." Tom looked at his mother and thought she was about to say something because she had such a funny look on her face, and maybe even tears in her eyes, but then she just nodded to Clint.

Suddenly, with a roar from the loudest engine he had ever heard, he felt the acceleration and they were off. He watched out to the side, behind Clint's broad back, and was absolutely in heaven. Soon enough he discovered that he could turn his head and see to both sides as they rode along heading out of town.

Tom was having so much fun turning his head back and forth that he was rocking the motorcycle from side to side and Clint had to tell him not to jump around so much. But he could hardly contain himself and the rocking back and forth continued, although at a slightly more subdued level. He knew most of the main streets around his small town, but moving swiftly on the motorcycle made him lose his bearings. Even so, he was in heaven and didn't care what road they were on.

He became aware of all the wonderful new movements he was feeling; the acceleration, the turns, the stopping, everything. It all felt wonderful. Soon he felt brave enough to peek around Clint's back so he could see where they were going and within minutes he began anticipating when the motorcycle was going to speed up or slow down or make a turn. He had never felt so happy.

They had been out for a quarter hour or so and Clint knew Wilma would be getting concerned, so he headed back. At first Tom felt quite disappointed when he saw the town coming into view down the long road ahead. But then within a few minutes he saw his mother standing there waiting and he felt so very anxious to tell her all about it. As soon as the motorcycle stopped and Clint helped him off, he happily ran to his mother and excitedly told her all about his fantastic adventure.

As soon as Clint had parked the motorcycle, Wilma reminded Tom to thank Mr. Larkins for the special birthday present. He ran and hugged Clint and thanked him over and over for the motorcycle ride. Then Clint walked over to her and said, "He sure had fun, and jumped back and forth the whole time. He rocked and rocked the motorcycle. I think I'll call him Rocky from now on. After he tripped over that big rock over there twice, and then rocked the motorcycle, it seems there's just no other name for him. Is that all right with you, Wilma?"

"What do you think, Tom?" she asked.

He didn't answer his mother because he was so busy yelling, "Yea! That's me! Rocky!"

It amazed Clint that his grand plan for Meredith was working so well, although he still felt nervous and scared around her. During study hall at school they had begun to sit together rather frequently as springtime arrived. Meredith seemed to really like having a boy around that wasn't hitting on her constantly or bragging about himself. And even though she was very bright, some school subjects were hard for her. He of course felt absolutely in heaven; there was nothing in the whole world he would rather be doing than sitting next to his dream girl. Well, perhaps there was one thing that would be better, but he tried very hard not to think about that when they were together. He was also very smart and together they could successfully tackle any school homework assignment. Meredith toned down her normal teasing for him, since he wasn't a typical boy that was after her, but she didn't or probably couldn't give it up completely. His quick wit and her gentle teasing played well toward each other, and they would frequently laugh out loud and then smile secretly at each other while being admonished by the teacher on monitor duty. Now that the two of them were together frequently in study hall, Phase 2 of the master plan was complete.

Sometimes one or two of Meredith's girlfriends would join them, which initially sent massive swells of fear through Clint, but then it began to set his heart on fire because he didn't know much about girl stuff but he suspected that if Meredith's friends didn't like him then he and his grand plan would be dead in the water. Apparently they found him to be harmless and he always made a point to be very helpful to all of them with their homework. This actually came naturally to him as his mother had taught him to always be helpful toward friend or family. So, then, as he gradually matured into a man, his mother's training had given him this great gift of being able to be helpful to not only the prettiest and most desirable girl in school but also to some of her friends, who were themselves pretty cute. Life was indeed good for Clint.

He had been trying to figure out what Phase 3 should be, when something momentous happened, so very momentous that he was completely flabbergasted when she said it. Clint and Meredith had just started working on an important history assignment that wasn't able to be completed in study hall alone. They were sitting side-by-side, as they frequently did, and as always Clint could sense her closeness with every nerve in his body. When she invited him to her house to work on the assignment together he didn't know what to do. He turned the brightest imaginable shade of red. He didn't know whether to die from embarrassment or jump for joy. What he did was sit frozen in the chair.

Meredith couldn't miss seeing that he turned bright red but with their history together she wasn't surprised at his periodic embarrassments, and she knew from her experiences with other boys that they also did that sometimes. It always made her feel good to know that she could have that effect on a boy, even if that time it was just Clint instead of a boy that was trying to impress her.

That was a Thursday and he went to her house that night, the next night, and lastly on Sunday afternoon. Clint suspected that she had been on a date Saturday night, but it would have been too painful for him to ever ask about such things and he only knew for sure what he overheard when Meredith was talking with her girl friends about their dating lives, but this time there had been no discussions that he could listen in on. One of those girl friends had the same assignment so she went to Meredith's home each time also, and they all got their assignments done early Sunday afternoon. That left part of the afternoon for listening to records, so they each chose one of their favorites from Meredith's collection and then they danced to them. It was that last part, the dancing, that gave Clint both the greatest and the worst things the boy had ever experienced in his life. It was the greatest because to dance with Meredith was to dance with heaven itself, whether a fast dance or the crème-de-la-crème of a slow dance. During the fast dances he got to watch her bouncing around, which was enough to give him pressure in the front of his pants, and he got to touch her hand to swing her around. How very fortunate he was to have a pre-teen younger sister that pleaded and cajoled him incessantly to dance with her so she could pretend to be a teenager. He was actually able to fast dance with Meredith and her girlfriend without feeling embarrassed about his skills, although it felt scary and nerve-wracking for him. And the girls loved having a boy to dance with instead of just dancing with each other. To his relief and also disappointment, those first songs had all been fast ones.

Mrs. Gold, Meredith's mom, brought out some refreshments for them and stayed to chat a few moments, but then disappeared again into the back of the house. Clint noticed that she was friendly to her daughter's guests, and evidently didn't want to interfere with their get-together by over staying in the living room. Mr. Gold wasn't home because Meredith's parents had just recently purchased Town Pharmacy and he had been putting in long hours changing the store around to the way they wanted it, including changing the name to Gold's Pharmacy. Since purchasing the business, Meredith had told Clint previously, they were seldom both home at the same time.

Shortly after Mrs. Gold delivered the refreshments and then left the teens alone, things went from scary for Clint and led straight to downright terror in a matter of about two seconds. The record player switched to a slow dance, and Meredith made no move to leave the open spot in her living room that had become their dance studio. He couldn't slow dance with her because the uncontrollable bulge in his pants that he had been able to hide up until that time would surely give itself away in a slow dance and then, to his utmost horror, might within moments wet the front of his pants while he ejaculated and hoped to die right there in a sudden and merciful death. He wondered how in the world he could possibly deal with this unexpected predicament. But he didn't have to wonder very long because the mere thought of holding Meredith up close started the familiar hormones and emotions racing through his body that he knew were the precursor to what he was dreading the most of all. He knew from all those nights in bed thinking about Meredith that once the sensations had escalated to that point he was going to come within moments even without stroking himself.

So, terror stricken, he lurched for the bathroom. Luckily it wasn't far away and he made it just in time to get his pants unzipped and grab a wad of toilet paper and reach into his pants, all the while fearing that he might also throw up from the terror of it all. Confused and befuddled, he had never experienced so many emotions in his life. He felt elated, relieved, terrified, sore in his stomach, very very embarrassed, and completely confused. But at least his erection was subsiding.

As soon as he felt able to, he splashed cold water on his face and the redness of embarrassment in his cheeks began fading away. Then he returned to the girls and a dream of his came true. He was able to slow dance with Meredith and actually held her somewhat up against himself in the process, which to his amazement, delight, and confusion, she didn't seem to mind at all.

After a few more records it was time to leave. He didn't know what the girls thought about his strange behavior when he had bolted away from them so abruptly, and he certainly wasn't going to mention it because he had no idea what he could say to explain it. What he didn't know was that they had giggled and laughed after he raced to the bathroom, not because they fully understood what had been going on, but simply because that's what young girls do. Fortunately they both thought he was a nice fellow so they didn't dwell on his strangeness very long. As for Clint, he went straight home and to his bathroom and repeated the very same activity that had been so embarrassing for him earlier. He then flopped on his bed and went instantly asleep; it had been quite a day.

After Clint left Meredith's house, her girl friend stayed a few minutes longer, then left for home. But not before the two of them talked about Clint, and Meredith confided in her girl friend that she liked Clint because he was witty and had a sense of humor, and was nice to her and didn't pester her for a date like so many boys did. She also confided that she had really liked being held by him when they had slow danced and hoped he was also interested in her and would soon ask her out.

FIVE

It was still early in the morning, too early, when Rocky finally walked into the edge of town. From the direction of his home, coming into town as he was, the main business area in Johnson's Crossing started abruptly after passing a farm on one side of the highway and a forested spot on the other side. Another block and a half brought him to the bench in front of Gold's Pharmacy, where he sat to await the rendezvous with his motorcycle. Clint had said to meet him there just before lunchtime.

He looked at his watch and realized, disappointedly, that he had several hours to go. Ever the daydreamer, his thoughts easily wandered back to his early history with Uncle Clint and the motorcycle. After that momentous ride on his seventh birthday, his mom had gradually allowed him to go for more and more frequent rides with Clint, but always insisting that the rides be kept to no longer than she planned to be shopping.

Clint was always happy to take him for a spin unless the pharmacy was too busy for him to get away.

Clint rode his motorcycle to work even during the winter, so long as the roads were clear of snow. But he was never willing to take Rocky for a ride unless the roads were safe and Mrs. Powlison trusted him in that way.

She loved seeing the joy and happiness in her son whenever he rode with Clint. She knew Rocky excitedly looked forward to her shopping trips and never missed a chance to accompany her into town. She trusted Clint completely and enjoyed seeing the two of them together having fun, especially since her son didn't have much fun at home. But she had to be careful and not let her husband Abe know about her frequent, although brief and innocent, encounters with Clint. And that meant Rocky could not tell his dad about the motorcycle rides.

Abe Powlison had worked at Johnson's Refinery for over twenty years. He had never risen above the level of General Maintenance Technician, largely because of his drinking and the problems it occasionally caused him at work, even though he never actually drank on the job. His saving grace with his supervisor was that he always showed up for work and didn't complain about the frequent shift changes that the maintenance crew had to bear. Even at his modest employment level, he was able to provide a simple but secure financial life for his wife and their son, and he had the prestige of working at the premier employer in the area.

Mrs. Powlison had to remind Rocky after every motorcycle ride that it would be best if his dad didn't know about the ride or about Mr. Larkins because he didn't like motorcycles or motorcycle riders. She hated that she had to lie to her husband, and really hated that she had to tell Rocky to lie to him also. But she couldn't risk what might happen when her husband drank too much and sometimes exploded irrationally. So it was the only way she and her son could continue to associate with Clint, and she couldn't bear the thought of losing that part of her and Rocky's lives.

That pattern continued until Rocky was 12 years old. About twice a week he and his mom went to town and always stopped in to see Clint, and most of the time there was a motorcycle ride in the offing. Rocky truly loved it, his mom was always happy when they saw Clint, and Clint loved taking Rocky for his adventures. Rocky's life revolved around the motorcycle rides and he felt ever so much happier, even at home.

Then one awful day Clint wasn't at the pharmacy. His mom spoke privately with one of the employees, then whisked Rocky out of the store and to their car, where she cried and cried for the longest time. She explained to Rocky that Mr. Larkins had a disease called cancer and that he wasn't feeling well and might not return to the pharmacy at all. Rocky cried too; it was the saddest day of his young life.

------- <<>> -------

Rocky would occasionally see Clint after that sad day, but the man wasn't the same anymore. He had stopped working at the pharmacy and didn't have a pattern that Rocky could figure out, so their meetings were haphazard. He would still take Rocky for an occasional motorcycle ride, but his ongoing pain and sadness seemed to have drained the joy from him.

Rocky always kept his eyes open whenever he was in town, and had seen that Clint was now living in a shack just off Main Street in a forested area. But he didn't feel comfortable in approaching the shack uninvited, so he never did. Meanwhile he did some reading about cancer so he would understand what Clint was going through, but that mostly just made him feel depressed so he stopped his research. He tried several times talking with his mom about Clint and his condition, but Wilma always changed the subject.

Over the years he noticed that Clint kept looking older and more weather-beaten, but felt unable to do anything about it. He knew about the cancer, but had no way of knowing that Clint was also still suffering from a broken heart, even though Meredith had been long ago in Clint's past.

Young Clint's love for Meredith took quite a giant leap after their slow dance late on that Sunday afternoon at her house. It gave him the push he needed to get past his fear of planning Phase 3 of his master plan to win over the girl of his dreams. It was fortuitous indeed that the very next Sunday he and his family went to visit his cousin Billy who had a farm an hour's drive out of town.

Billy had been clearing out his shed to make room for a new tractor and wanted to give away a motor scooter that he didn't have space for anymore. Clint had ridden the scooter a few times and loved it so he jumped at the chance to have it, and his parents OK'd the deal. He rode the machine home and immediately set about cleaning and polishing everything on it. Now his thoughts were mixed between his new scooter and Meredith, with the girl, as always, never being more than a moment away from occupying his full mind.

While polishing the paint on his scooter, in a flash of inspiration he realized what Phase 3 of his master plan would be. He would sweep Meredith away on his new prized scooter and show her that he was more fun than any of the other boys at school. Phase 3 would then conclude with their sharing a kiss. Unfortunately, the mere thought of putting a kiss into Phase 3 made him feel faint and he had to sit down for a time. He decided that the kiss would wait for Phase 4. Or perhaps Phase 5 or 6.

Nope, Phase 3 is where the kiss happens. Courage and bravery are, after all, honorable and valuable virtues. It's time to press onwards before she decides she likes someone else.

Monday arrived and with it Clint's fear returned. He didn't know what kind of affair he could ask Meredith to so that she wouldn't think he was asking her on a date. He still felt that if she thought he was trying to date her she would be repulsed and tell him to take a permanent hike.

Fortunately she solved his problem for him by asking him over to her house on Friday evening for a pre-slumber party get together. She explained to him that she would be hosting a slumber party for her girl friends and that her parents had agreed that they could invite boys over earlier in the evening. And that she would like to dance with him again. As usual, Clint was speechless but he did manage to do an affirmative nod before he bolted away from her, his stomach in knots of fear and nervousness.

Over the next few days he spent a lot of time praying that he wouldn't embarrass himself at Meredith's party.

He arrived at her house at the appointed time on his shiny scooter, but parked it out of sight because he wanted to control the timing of the surprise of it all. There were several of Meredith's girl friends there, most of whom knew Clint fairly well from study hall and so felt comfortable with him and even welcomed him, especially the ones that knew Meredith was interested in him.

There were also several handsome boys from school, every one of whom was very surprised to see him at the home of the school's most beautiful girl. Not one of the boys knew why Clint had been invited, but they whispered amongst themselves and decided it must be because he spent time with Meredith in study hall and she must feel sorry for him and so invited him out of pity. They couldn't fathom the idea that one of these girls, the school's prettiest, might have invited him because of some romantic interest.

Meredith told everybody that both of her parents were still at the pharmacy because of some problem that had come up, but would be home before it was time for the boys to leave. A couple of the boys took that as permission to retrieve some beer from their car, but they could only talk Meredith into allowing four cans into the house. So they all passed around the beers, with many of them naively thinking that eleven people drinking four beers would make them all completely drunk.

What it did do, however, was make them all feel giddy and free. Not from the alcohol but simply from thinking they were getting drunk. Everyone was dancing and having a good time, with two or three couples trying to hide in out of the way places, kissing and hugging. Meredith and her closest friends were very firm about everyone staying fairly close to the living room and not allowing anything to go on that would get her in trouble when her parents got home later.

What am I doing here? I don't fit in with those people. If I go over to any of them they'll just tell me I don't belong here and to leave. Where can I hide? Maybe I should just leave. I could easily get away without anyone noticing. Meredith's not paying attention to me and probably wouldn't even miss me. Those three guys are following her around like puppy dogs. She'll dance with them before me. Here I go again, back to the kitchen. Then it'll be back to the living room. Then back to the kitchen. Why did she invite me anyway? Where can I hide? Everyone else has danced a lot already and I'm just standing around looking dumb. But wait a minute - she hasn't danced at all. Why not? Those puppy dogs must have been asking her. Why isn't she dancing with any of them? Strange. Maybe I should wait a little while before slipping away. Just to see what she does next.

Once the hyper level of activity settled down Meredith broke away from the three boys and walked straight over to Clint and took him to the only place available for them to sit down, in an over-stuffed easy chair. She told him to sit down then she squeezed in next to him. He instinctively scooted over as far as he could, but even so the chair wasn't really wide enough for the two of them. Undeterred, Meredith pressed herself into the chair and sat tightly beside him. He heard her talking to him, but he couldn't follow her words because he thought he was going to faint or die, or both. But he did manage to barely stay coherent enough to give the appearance of being alive.

After a time Clint was able to focus enough to follow the conversation that she had unknowingly, up until then, been having with herself. He even started responding, barely, in his usual witty way and she laughed several times.

Meanwhile, every boy in the room and a few of the girls had no idea whatsoever of what in the world was going on. What could Meredith be doing with, of all people, Clint? But a few of her closest girl friends knew very well what she was up to, and they giggled seeing how nervous Clint looked. The other girls and all of the boys just looked bewildered. Then someone turned the brightest of the living room lights off which took the two of them out of the spotlight, so to speak.

By that time Clint was pretty much on automatic pilot. Never in his life had he been so close to a girl, any girl, and now the one-and-only girl that made him weak in the knees pressed tightly against his side. It was all entirely too much. He couldn't consciously deal with the massive feelings and emotions that were running rampant through his body and mind, so he just sort of checked out and left the autopilot in control. He felt as if he were outside of his body and everything just went on in a normal way while he watched from above. He even felt fairly peaceful, but in a funny sort of way. He actually wondered why he hadn't been able to use this technique before; it would have made all of his interactions with Meredith so much easier.

Their conversation in the easy chair continued for several long minutes until he had the idea that since she willingly sat there pressing against him, she might actually agree to slow dance with him. It would be a risk just to ask her, but he thought the odds of success were reasonably high and the odds of going down in flames and embarrassment were low. So he waited impatiently until the music changed to a good selection and then asked her to dance. Thankfully she immediately agreed and jumped right up from the chair.

Neither of them noticed the shocked look on some of the other faces when they started to dance closely against each other. Meredith had decided that he was so inexperienced with girls the only way to see if he had an interest in her would be to let him know she was interested in him. So that's just what she was going to do. She pressed against him and instead of taking his left hand with her right hand, she put both arms up around his neck. Clint knew that girls only took this position if they liked the boy they were dancing with, but his automatic pilot seemed to ignore it and just proceeded to dance as if nothing earth shattering had just happened. This was indeed fortunate, as the real Clint would have reacted totally inappropriately and run away to upchuck or done something else dumb or embarrassing.

But even his autopilot couldn't keep from getting an erection, and with her curves pressed so close up against him it would be impossible to hide it from her. He pretended it wasn't happening and just kept dancing and making small talk, all the while wondering when she was going to slap him and evict him forever from her life. But none of that happened. The most beautiful girl he had ever seen stayed pressed to him and kept dancing. When the music ended she moved slightly away while waiting for the next song, which turned out to be another slow song. When she moved back into his arms, even his autopilot had trouble maintaining control.

There was a commotion and people were stirring around the room, and they realized that Meredith's parents were just driving up. She quickly reached up and kissed him right on the lips, lingering for a moment, then pulled away to go greet her parents. After that it was time for the boys to leave.

He was in a daze all the way home and could barely control his motor scooter. *I don't believe it! Did she actually kiss me? In front of everyone? I must be dreaming! Or hallucinating. Maybe I've pined after her so long I've gone crazy. I'm worse than those puppy dog boys following her around. The kiss didn't really happen. I'm just imagining it all. But I'm not. I can still feel it. She pressed into me and didn't pull back from my hard-on. Why? Then she kissed me! Even after feeling it against her. What's going on? Why didn't I kiss her back? The chance of a lifetime and I blew it. My plan's working out perfectly and now I've screwed it all up. She must think I don't like her. Now she'll never give me a chance to show her how much I love her. She must think I made a fool of her. I couldn't have been any dumber. But why did she dance only with me? And why did she kiss me?*

There was one thing for sure: his plan for Phase 3 had just taken a giant leap.

SIX

Rocky had been sitting on the bench in front of Gold's Pharmacy for almost an hour. His daydreams kept him occupied, as they always did. But even so, the minutes were passing painfully slowly while he waited for the appointed time to meet with Uncle Clint to get "his" new motorcycle.

He saw his mother drive by but it didn't register for a few moments because he was lost in thought. Then it hit his awareness and startled him into complete alertness. It was her bible study day and she wouldn't have any reason to drive through town instead of going straight from home to church. Not only that, but he had told her he was going up to Old Maid's Creek so he shouldn't be in town either. So there they both were, where they weren't supposed to be. Luckily she hadn't noticed him, but he wanted to see where she was going so he ran down the sidewalk trying to keep her car in sight.

She pulled into the lot beside Fran's Fabrics and parked at the very rear of the lot near the forest. He hid behind a truck that was parked across the street from

Fran's and watched his mother. She had a grocery bag with her when she exited the car but instead of going into Fran's she looked around quickly and then walked rapidly behind the store. His curiosity had now skyrocketed and he had to see where she was going, even at the risk of exposing his presence, so he ran across the street to the rear corner of the building and furtively peeked around the corner.

She was disappearing rapidly down the path in the forest that he knew led to Uncle Clint's shack. He had seen Clint go down that path a couple of times when Clint didn't know he was being watched, and Rocky had scouted it himself once when Clint was elsewhere in town. This whole thing with his mom was quite a surprise, indeed. He couldn't imagine what she was up to, but he did know he'd better get out of sight so she wouldn't see him when she returned. So he went back to Gold's and hid beside the building, knowing his mother would drive by shortly on her way back toward the church.

"Good morning," she said with a big smile. "How are you today?"

Clint looked up from wiping the morning dew off of the motorcycle and smiled at Wilma. Then he lied and told her, "I'm chipper and dandy, just like always. And how are you this fine spring morning?"

"Well I'm just chipper and dandy too, and always happy to see you my dear friend. I've brought you some meatloaf and vegetables. Oh, and also one of my homemade apple tarts. So, I see you're getting her ready for Rocky. Today's sure a big day for both of you. How are you feeling about that?"

"Rotten. Pretty rotten. And very sad and depressed. And angry too, I suppose. I feel like I'm betraying Meredith's memory, but I know this is the right thing to do now. Rocky's finally old enough and I need to let go of my dear old love. There's also something else I want to tell you. I've been thinking about going on down to Roanoke after Rocky buys her and getting some of that cancer treatment you told me about."

Wilma ran over and hugged the unwashed older man and kissed him all over the stubbles on his dirty face but she didn't care how dirty he was or how much he smelled. "Hooray!!!" she shouted. "Oh Clint, you've just made me the happiest woman in the world! Thank you thank you thank you!"

They hugged for a long time, with Clint feeling the warmth that had endured for so many years whenever he saw her. Even though they only visited together for brief moments, he felt as if they had loved each other for a very long time.

Finally, after they had released the hug, she told him that she had not let on to Rocky that she knew about his impending motorcycle purchase, and that she still planned to let it be his secret until he felt ready to tell her himself. Then she told him, "Meredith loved you. She would want you to move on and let go of the painful memories. Oh, I so want that for you also. You deserve to be happy and it pains me so much to see you always so sad and lonely. It's time for Teaser to pass to Rocky now, and for you to get fixed up in Roanoke."

They briefly discussed when and how he would get to Roanoke, then he told her, "I'm going to tell him about college today, Wilma. I just don't know how long I have left in this world and I want to tell him now just in case I don't make it back from Roanoke."

Her face turned ashen and her body went stiff as a board. She had known for some time now that he planned to tell Rocky, but even so it shocked her to finally hear the actual words. She was so grateful for what Clint wanted to do for Rocky, but she knew it would bring up some very big problems to be dealt with.

"I have a favor to ask," he said, bringing her back into the moment. "There's something inside, I'll get it. Please say yes to the favor." Before Wilma could respond he had disappeared into his shack, returning to her in barely a moment. He set a small steamer trunk down in front of her and opened it.

Looking quizzically inside, she wasn't sure what it all meant. After a few moments she asked, "May I look?"

"Yes, of course. Here, these were taken at our wedding." He handed her an old, yellowed photo album filled with pictures of him and Meredith at their wedding. Wilma was born after Meredith had died, but she had seen a few pictures of the beautiful young woman. Now here was an entire photo album brimming with pictures, showing how happy the couple looked together. She felt a moment of jealousy but immediately pushed it out of her mind; it had all been, after all, long before she was even born. She looked at a few pages of pictures, then carefully returned the album to its place in the trunk.

"These are clearly very special to you," she said. "I had no idea you even had them, or that you could have saved them all these years out here in the woods. Why are you showing them to me now?"

"There's a couple more photo albums, including some early pictures with me and my sister before pneumonia got her in 1950. But there's more than that." He paused, then continued, "Meredith always kept a diary. That's what these other books are. They're from when she first moved here from Atlanta, right up until just before she died. She told me her older diaries, the ones from before she moved here, somehow got lost in the move from Atlanta. After she died I just couldn't bring myself to destroy these. They seemed too intimate, too much a part of her. Then I realized that she would have wanted me to have them. That it would help keep her alive, so to speak."

He paused to wipe away the tears that had started streaming down his face, then continued, "I can't just leave them here while I'm in Roanoke. There's no telling what might happen to my old shack here. That's why I'm asking you to keep them safe for me until I come back," pausing, he again dried his face and eyes. "So I want you to take this trunk with you now."

Wilma didn't hesitate even a moment before telling him, "Of course, my darling, you know I'll protect them for you." She knew he had no living siblings or close cousins, making her and Rocky the only "family" the man knew, so there was no one else to safeguard his heritage. Besides, she felt very special that he would entrust Meredith's history to her.

"There's one more thing," he said. "I want you to look at the pictures sometimes, and also to read the diaries. They're so very personal to Meredith, but wherever she is I know she can see how special and important you are to me, and I can just feel that she would be honored that I want to share her with you in this way. And then her memory can live on even if I don't make it back from Roanoke. She was such a wonderful and loving person, she deserves to be remembered like that."

Rocky couldn't make sense of what he had just seen. The only thing he could think of that made any sense at all was that his mother had taken some food to Uncle Clint, which would explain why he sometimes couldn't find some particularly favorite leftover in the refrigerator. If that's what she was doing, why keep it a secret?

No sooner had he asked himself that question than he knew the answer. Of course she would have to keep it a secret. If his dad found out there would be an awful explosion and she would surely get hit. He knew his mom had always been happy when they saw Uncle Clint at Gold's, so he supposed they were friends and she wanted to help him now that he didn't seem able to take good care of himself. *Dad never seemed to particularly like Uncle Clint. So that must be it, then. Mom's kind hearted and takes food to him. Yep, that's what it is. Well, I'm sure not gonna let that cat out of the bag.*

He was very careful to never do anything that he thought might lead to a blow-up from his father. Sometimes it happened anyway after Dad had been drinking too much, and he'd usually get hit a couple of times, but for sure he wasn't going to knowingly cause it. Especially in a situation like this where Mom would take the brunt of dad's anger.

Thinking about all of it just hardened his determination to run away as soon as he had saved a little more money. Just him and his motorcycle. That would also help his mom, he naively believed, because when his father had been drinking too much and started yelling at Mom oftentimes it included Rocky's name and she always had to defend him. So if he just ran away then his dad wouldn't have him to get angry at and then yell and sometimes hit Mom.

After Wilma left, Clint's thoughts went back to his courtship of Meredith. *It's been decades now, but I still can't quite believe she would ever like a plain fellow such as me. Especially with every good-looking boy in school trying to get her. But I beat them all, didn't I? Those puppy dogs following her around sure got a hell of a surprise.*

She loved new and wild things, that's for sure. Sometimes I'd overhear her talking with a girlfriend and she was always excited when talking about some new adventure. But I saw that other side of her, the soft and tender side, and I just knew she wasn't wild in a bad sense at all.

Boys would sometimes brag that they had gotten into her, and he sometimes knew that she had been on a date with a particular boy, even though she dated only a few of them. Those stories always hurt him right to the core, but his gut feeling told him they were always lies. She never had a steady, and if a boy had been lucky enough to make some progress with her it only made sense that he would want to go steady with her so he could make even more progress. He reckoned that meant no steady equaled no progress. At least he fervently hoped that's what it meant.

He had never seen her show any special affection to any boy in school, even the ones that he knew had been on a date with her. It was true that she always flirted with boys, and loved teasing with them. But even though they congregated around her at every opportunity, which she seemed to encourage, he never saw her do anything more than touch a boy on the arm or chest. Of course, coming from a beauty like her that was enough to keep a boy hanging around for a long time. But a touch wasn't a kiss, and he had never seen her kiss anyone. Except for himself. And he had no idea what to make of that or what to do about it. What he needed was a new plan for Phase 3.

But he couldn't figure out anything for a new plan because he didn't know what the evening at Meredith's had meant. And he was so inexperienced with girls that he had nothing to fall back on for inspiration. He couldn't ask his younger sister because then she would know he was sweet on Meredith and besides he thought she was still too young to know about such things. So he was just plain stumped. Phase 3 wasn't going to happen until he figured things out.

Over the rest of the weekend he had worried with his problem, then decided to take his scooter to school on Monday and hide it so no one would know about it, and to offer Meredith a ride home after school but not to let on what type of transport he had planned for her. He figured that his chances of success were quite high since she had kissed him, but there was still a chance of getting shot down because he had so stupidly not responded to her and had just stood there like a dork. Over the weekend he took his sister for several rides on the scooter so he could practice how to handle it with a passenger on board, preparing hopefully for Meredith, of course.

Meanwhile, he couldn't have known what transpired at Meredith's slumber party after he and the other boys left. Immediately, all of the girls grilled her incessantly about her and Clint. It didn't take them long to get the information they wanted from their hostess. Some of them were so flabbergasted that she could like Clint, out of all the boys at school, that they just didn't believe her and figured that she was lying to cover up some scheme she was cooking up. But her best friends supported her and told her not to worry that he hadn't responded to her kiss because he was surely quite surprised by it all, and that she should just wait and see how he acted toward her at school on Monday. Meredith wasn't convinced.

Monday came, and they saw each other in the hall at school just before homeroom started. *I have to ask her right away. If I wait I'll lose my nerve. How do*

I say it? Will she accept? What if she's upset about the kiss on Friday? Maybe she'll tell me I'm horrible and to get away from her. No, she wouldn't be that mean. But she might say no anyway. Here goes. "Can I give you a ride home after school today?" Then he remembered what his mother always told him about thanking people so he quickly added, "Oh, I almost forgot, thank you for asking me over on Friday. I really, really enjoyed it."

Meredith's heart jumped and she immediately accepted. *Wow! That's sure a surprise. A ride home? Of course we can ride home together. There he goes, gone already. He sure likes to get away fast sometimes. Whoops, I forgot to ask how he got a car. Oh well, I like surprises so this is good.*

For Clint, the day passed more slowly than any day in his life had ever done before. For Meredith, her anticipation about being with Clint and her curiosity about his car kept her excited all day.

When Meredith realized that she was about to get a ride on a motor scooter she wildly exclaimed, "This is fantastic! I've never been on a cycle before! Wow! How did you ever get this?"

Clint explained about his cousin Billy, then put their books in the saddlebags and they hopped on. She swiftly pulled her skirt around her legs, just above her knees, which gave Clint a thrill because he had never seen above her calves before. Then she hugged up against his back and put her arms around him and they were off. Clint asked if she would like to ride around some before going to her house and she excitedly told him, "Yes, yes, yes!"

At first, he could barely control the scooter with Meredith on the bike also. He had the brief experiences carrying his sister, but his balance wasn't skilled yet. That was only part of his problem. With the beautiful young woman snuggled up against him all he could feel was her chest and breasts pressing into his back, her thighs on either side of his buttocks, and her arms wrapped tightly around his waist. The thought of her thighs opening around him was almost more than he could take. It took every bit of concentration and skill he had to keep from crashing, but he managed, barely, to avoid disaster. Then, mercifully, after a few minutes the sensations he was feeling from her closeness lost a tad of their intensity and he was able to function somewhat better. She seemed so excited at riding on his bike with him that he didn't think she noticed his lack of skill or how distracted her physical touch made him.

About 45 minutes later they arrived at her house. He had decided that on their first outing he shouldn't stop anywhere along the way because he was nervous and it would be best to just get her home safely. Going to her house would be awkward enough if she invited him inside, especially if her parents were both still at the Pharmacy. Naturally she invited him to come in.

Once inside, she looked around then told him, "My parents aren't home yet, but they've both met you so they won't mind you being here. Let's see if we can find any snacks in the kitchen." A few minutes later they were freshly armed with sandwiches and drinks and were sitting at the kitchen table talking about his motor scooter. She was thrilled that he had taken her for a new adventure and quickly let him know that she hoped they could do it again real soon, so they set a date for Wednesday after school, since she had cheerleader practice Tuesday afternoon and her mom would pick her up afterwards.

They were having fun just talking and after a while Mrs. Gold came home and started dinner, so he left for his own house. As he was leaving Meredith came out onto the porch with him and closed the door so her mom couldn't see them and put her arms up around his neck and kissed him. He hadn't been expecting that, although secretly he had thought it would be wonderful if they kissed again. But he hadn't dared to seriously consider the possibility. He did, however, manage to rise to the occasion and put his arms around her and kiss her back.

To Clint it felt like their first kiss together, since the first time he hadn't really participated, and the thrill of it all shot through him like lightning. He tingled so much it felt as if all of his hair was standing straight out from his skin. His knees were weak. His groin went into shock. His lips couldn't get enough of the softness of her luscious and full lips. His arms wanted to hold her forever. Then, after a few moments, she pulled back from him and pressed her hand against his chest for a moment, then disappeared quickly into her house.

He fell down the steps as he was leaving her porch. Then he fell off his scooter before he had gone more than a dozen yards. Luckily he fell onto the dirt beside the road and wasn't hurt. He took a wrong turn, then another wrong turn, then ran a stop sign, then the motor died because he had forgotten to open the gas petcock. When he finally made it home, he accidentally let the scooter fall over to the side while he was getting off. He tripped going up the steps to his room. Finally, mercifully, he fell onto his bed and just laid there in a semi-conscious daze.

SEVEN

A noise in the woods brought the old man back to reality, pulling him away from his memories of Meredith. At first he thought Wilma had returned, but then he saw, as he often did, a deer walking by. He turned back to Teaser and realized that he had wiped her off completely and she was dry from the morning dew. The sun had been up for a while and he figured she had warmed enough that he could get her started. The older he got, the harder it was for him to start the gleaming machine. He could still stand on the starter lever and give the girl a good hard kick, but his body now always gave him a substantial protest.

This will be our last ride, old girl. You know I love you, but young Rocky will covet you like I have. It's time for you to have a younger man astride you. Let him feel your power, your roar. I'll try to see you from time to time, but he'll take good care of you. You need to take good care of him, too. He's not yet wise about women, so you be gentle with him, you hear?

She had never left him like Meredith did, never tore his heart out from his still breathing chest. His sadness felt deeply profound and for a moment he thought he shouldn't pass her along to Rocky. But his frequent thoughts like that were always fleeting because he knew the time had come. Teaser would be Rocky's now, and rightfully so. It was time to go on down to Roanoke and get medical help. Maybe, just maybe, his cancer could still be cured and he might be fortunate enough to see Rocky grow into a man. The appointment at the cancer treatment hospital had already been set. And, he reminded himself, it's what Wilma wanted him to do and he wanted to please her. Now he just had to go through the motions until he got himself there.

It had long been his plan to take a nice, leisurely ride on Teaser that last morning, and that's just what he was going to do. He turned on the ignition, opened the gas petcock, raised the starter lever to the up position, and then lunged downwards on the starter with all his might. Nothing happened. How could he have forgotten the choke lever? Oh well, he thought, I'll just do it again. This time the mighty machine roared into exuberant life and Clint, as he always did, felt the rumble of her exhaust through his entire body. What a wonderful feeling it was, a feeling he had never grown tired of. His girl never failed to give him a thrill.

Off he went. Down the path to the parking lot beside Fran's Fabrics, then to the street and straight out of town. The thrill of the road filled his thoughts. The wind in his hair, what was left of it, anyway, felt wonderful. The highway disappearing in his rearview mirror always gave him a visual thrill unlike anything else he had ever experienced. He twisted the throttle open wider and the mighty girl roared beneath him and leaped forward. That was what he had lived for the last decade, and she never failed to deliver for him. The phone poles raced past, the farmer's fences came and went, the dense forest took over and within minutes he was heading deep into the green walls of trees that lined both sides of the rural highway. He began turning one way then the other as the road started up into the foothills of the Blue Ridge Mountains. His hands knew instinctively how to twist the throttle just the right amount for each hill, and how far to turn the handlebars for each undulation of the old highway.

Higher and higher they went, man and machine, until the warmth of the valley was lost to the penetrating chill of the mountain air. He was getting cold, then colder, then to the point of being too cold to continue any higher. He stopped at an overlook and immediately felt warmer without the wind whistling through his clothes. He walked and climbed a bit and sat on the same boulder that he and Meredith had sat upon so many times, looking over the lush green valley below. He knew this would be the last time he and Teaser would be here together, although he hoped that Rocky would bring her up here sometimes.

The tears started slowly, but were soon coming in torrents. He missed Meredith more than life itself. Then, eventually, somewhere deep inside he realized that missing her more than even his own life was probably why he felt so sad and depressed all the time, and maybe even why he had cancer now. That thought didn't stop the tears right away, but it did start to lessen the pain and the intensity of his crying. As he stopped crying, he began to realize that it was time to let go of Meredith and Teaser both. Otherwise, he would die a sad old man with nothing left to live for.

That's just not going to happen. I'm going to be alive to see Rocky grow into a man, and that's that. There's just one more thing I have to do before meeting him later, so I'd better start back down the mountain.

------- <<>> -------

There goes Mom on her way to church, just like I thought would happen. It's safe now. I can come out of hiding and sit in front of Gold's. I wonder whatever's going on with her and Uncle Clint. It must be that she takes food to him, but it still seems sort of strange. I wish I knew what seems so troubling about it.

There it is! I hear it. My machine's rumble! What a wondrous sound she makes. Wait! It's going the wrong way. Where's Uncle Clint taking my motorcycle? They're headed out of town! But that can't be – he's supposed to bring her over here to Gold's. Why would he be headed the wrong way? Did he change his mind? He wouldn't do that, would he? There they go, down the road straight away from me. Damn. What's going on? Wait a minute. It's still early, much earlier than we agreed on. So he must be going out for a last ride. At least I sure hope that's what's going on.

He decided to get a snack and headed inside Gold's to their grocery and convenience items section. At least that would take his mind off what had just happened.

------- <<>> -------

Clint parked Teaser just outside the old rickety wood fence. He stayed on the saddle for a while, feeling very apprehensive at the prospect of what he had to do now. It couldn't be put off any longer, he knew, and he sure wasn't looking forward to it.

The old gate stood there open, as if it were calling him to come on through. Even though the gate probably hadn't been closed in years, to him it seemed like it had just opened and beckoned to him. *It's now or never. She's been waiting in there for me a very long time now. Guess I'll just see how she's doing.* With that thought, he walked through the gate and into the cemetery that he had avoided for decades.

No matter that it had been 39 years since his last visit, he still knew exactly where to find her. The tears were pouring down his face by the time he walked up to the handcrafted headstone that he had personally designed so long ago. The inscription had dirt in it because no one had been there in so long to care for it, but he could still read it even through his tears: "Meredith Larkins" it said, "1930 – 1960", and "Beautiful Person, Loving Wife and Treasured Daughter. You Will Be Cherished Always".

For a long time he just stood there, thinking back to their life together. He recalled how happy they and everyone else had been when they married, which happened right out of high school. How she had moved with him to Roanoke where they both went to college and worked part-time, even though her parents were generous with help. How he had become a pharmacist and she had studied marketing and accounting, although the colleges made it difficult for a woman in those days. Despite whatever struggles they had, their college years together had been absolutely wonderful. After college their married life was still wonderful together. Until, that is, the horrible day when she left him forever.

He sat down on the unkempt mix of weeds and wild grass next to the gravestone, but not on Meredith's grave area itself. He remembered how, so many years ago, their romance had almost been stopped even before it could really get going. They had made plans to go to a movie on the very next Friday night after their first motor scooter ride together; it would be their first official date. Then on Friday morning in school she came up to him, looking very distraught, and told him her parents wouldn't let her go out with him because he wasn't Jewish.

He hadn't known she was Jewish, nor had he even really known very much about what that meant. The preacher down at the church always taught tolerance of other people and their beliefs, saying that setting a good example was the godly way to act, and his attitude had influenced many of the townsfolk. So Clint hadn't been exposed to very much anti-Semitism and didn't know much about Judaism. But he did know enough to then realize that Meredith's somewhat exotic looks must have come from her Jewish heritage. But whatever her heritage, it wasn't a reason for them not to be together and he intended to tell Mr. and Mrs. Gold that right to their faces.

Meredith stopped him cold in his tracks and told him in very firm tones that he had to do this her way if he had any hope at all of ever taking her out. She went on to explain that she had dated a few non-Jewish boys from school but that her parents had become increasingly insistent that she only date Jews. Since there were only a very, very few Jewish boys in school, that had pretty much eliminated her dating life, she said. Besides, she reassured him, it was him she wanted to go out with, not any other boys. But there was some hope with her parents because she had talked them into having him over for dinner on Sunday so they could get to know him better. For now, she insisted, that was the best that could be done.

His heart was broken. He had worked so hard to get to that point, then it was all shot down because of an unforeseen circumstance that he had no control over. The weekend began with him feeling lost and empty inside, and profoundly sad. His stomach hurt and he had no appetite, but wouldn't answer his mother's query about why he wasn't eating his breakfast. Finally, while Saturday wore on, he began to consider how lucky he was that Meredith really wanted to go out with him and that she had gotten them a possible reprieve. So, he told himself, count your blessings instead of moping around so sad.

Sunday came and went, as did the dinner with Meredith's parents. He felt that it had gone really well because he had been polite and they had engaged him in conversation throughout the dinner. He had liked the meal and asked for seconds, which really seemed to please Mrs. Gold. Mr. Gold had talked about dating and had asked him how much dating experience he had, which was very embarrassing because he had to confess in front of Meredith that he had none at all, which fortunately didn't seem to bother her. The Gold's had asked lots of questions about his family, his motor scooter, and his grades in school. Meredith jumped in and told them about all the time she and Clint had spent together in study hall and that they had both gotten good grades in their shared classes because of studying together, which seemed to please her parents a lot.

But unfortunately he left after dinner not knowing if there was any chance left for him and Meredith. His sadness returned to fill the void he felt in his heart and chest, and his queasy stomach re-announced itself with a vengeance.

------- <<>> -------

Clint carefully cleaned the dirt from the gravestone and pulled the weeds that were all around it. He noticed that some of the graves were well kept and wondered if their loved ones came by regularly to visit.

Then, without quite realizing what he was doing, he began talking to Meredith. "My darling," he said, through the tears that again began to dampen his eyes and face, "I've missed you so very much. We were so happy together. Why oh why did you leave me like you did? I've been so sad for so many years, so empty, so completely empty. I've been angry at you for leaving but now I know it's finally time to let go of all that. I'm trying really hard now to forgive myself for how I've been these last decades."

"Someday I'll join you right here and I can hardly wait to be with you again. But there's something else first, my dearest love. I want to tell you about a young lad named Rocky."

He proceeded to tell her everything about Rocky, then Teaser, and all about his life for the past 39 years, including his plans about going to Roanoke for cancer treatment. He laid down on the weeds and grass and rolled over atop her grave, and the tears again came in buckets. After a time the tears stopped and he told her, "I'm going now, to meet up with Rocky. Oh, by the way, I'm charging him $182 for Teaser. You remember why, don't you?" He continued, "Well, bye for now. I'll come to see you again when I get back from Roanoke. I love you. Always have."

As he was walking sadly and slowly away a man drove up and gathered some gardening tools from the back of his pickup truck and headed into the graveyard.

When they were close enough he spoke to the man and they exchanged hellos. Clint was somewhat surprised that the man didn't back away with a look of disgust at the sight and smell of the disheveled old man. Most of the townsfolk always did, even the ones Clint had known for many years. He guessed the fellow had been making a minimal living from odd jobs for years, and probably wasn't too choosy about the company he kept. But that didn't really matter to Clint, for there was something he had to know from the man; he asked, "Do you take care of someone's grave in particular?"

"No, not no one special for me, anyways. Some of them families pays me to keep the graves lookin good. I comes by every month, more in summer, and spruces em up. Reckon it gives them that's livin some peace of mind. Don't rightly know whatever them dead folks thinkin bout it, though."

Without hesitation Clint engaged the man to keep Meredith's grave in good shape, along with the adjacent graves of Mr. and Mrs. Gold, signing up for the most expensive service the fellow offered, telling him who to see at the bank in town to arrange for payment. Clint left the graveyard feeling lighter and happier than he had in years. *That fellow's right. It gives peace of mind to the living. It'll be real nice knowing Meredith's got a nice place to rest.*

The mighty machine seemed to come alive like it hadn't for many years. He could feel the engine's vibration between his legs and under his buttocks. He felt alive, more so than he could remember, and Teaser responded to him in kind. Together they rode away from the graveyard and back toward town, with the exhaust pipes roaring and the highway disappearing rapidly in the rear view mirrors. He loved the wind in his face and the weather was perfect for the ride. For a few minutes he even forgot that a fateful rendezvous awaited them both.

EIGHT

Wilma had packed up a nice bag of meatloaf and vegetables earlier that morning. Also one of her special apple tarts that she had saved from the day before and kept hidden from Rocky and her husband. She always packed these special delivery bags very carefully, and put in only the best of her home cooked meals. After all, the recipient of her lovingly prepared gifts was someone very special to her.

Every Wednesday morning she made up a bag, and if her husband Abe happened to be on day shift she also did one on Friday morning. Wednesday's were easy because she always went to her Bible study meeting and potluck at the church even if Abe was home. But she had to be careful on Fridays because he sometimes hassled her about leaving the house, and she also couldn't risk having the food bag discovered. It didn't matter to Abe if they needed groceries or if she had errands to do, since he didn't need much of an excuse to act irrationally or aggressively toward her. But at least he didn't usually drink in the mornings, even if he was working the night shift, so sometimes on the

Fridays that he was home she could still pack a food bag and get away for a bit.

For Wilma those weren't errands of mercy, but of love. Her dearest friend Clint wasn't able to take care of himself and had been that way for many years. So she made sure he got a personal visit from her and some home cooking once or twice a week and she would keep on doing so. In Wilma's mind and heart her trips to visit Clint and take him food were just as important as taking care of her son, and they were even more important than what her husband wanted.

She kept a careful check on the class schedule at Fran's Fabrics to make sure she wouldn't be in the parking lot when a class was about to start or just letting out. That way she minimized the possibility of being seen. If she was planning to stay at Clint's only briefly then she would sometimes park in Fran's lot, but usually she parked on the street and walked through the parking lot to the entrance to Fran's, which happened to be located at the rear of the lot. She would then just walk quickly on past and duck behind the building within moments, and if it was a Wednesday she always returned in time to get to her Bible study class. That subterfuge had worked successfully for many years. Wilma had, in fact, become so confident in her secret trips that she didn't notice her son watching her on that particular Wednesday morning.

Teaser rolled into the gas station and was brought to a stop in front of the old pump.

The hand-written sign on the window said Gus was out doing a tire change and would be back shortly. Some years back Gus had been forced to turn off the pumps when he was out on service calls; before that he just left them on and people would leave money for their gas purchases. But the state environmental department said it was a safety hazard to leave the pumps on while unattended, so Gus now turned them off. Clint, like most of Gus's friends and long-time customers, knew the switch location and could have turned on the pumps, but he decided to wait for Gus since there was still plenty of time before his meeting with Rocky.

He sat on one of the rickety old wooden beach chairs that Gus kept in front of the office. His favorite had always been the one closest to the edge of the building, which afforded him the easiest escape around the corner of the structure if too many people pulled into the gas station at one time. Although that hadn't happened but a few times, it still gave him a feeling of security to be able to get away from any gathering of people. So, as always, he sat on the end chair.

He tried to keep his thoughts from returning to Meredith. But then he realized that what he had been doing the last few days was different from how he usually thought about her. Ever since she had been taken from him so unexpectedly, oh so many years ago, he had always focused on how sad he felt no matter what the memory or how much pleasure might otherwise have been inherent in it. But something was very different. He supposed it could be because it was time to move forward, and the chronological processing he had recently been doing was more of a release than anything else. As he went through moments of their history together, he wasn't feeling the same kind of sadness as before. Sadness was still there, and plenty of it, but now he didn't seem to be dwelling on it, and he wasn't getting stuck in any particular memory. Instead, thankfully, he was going through time and letting go of much sadness.

Relief surged through him like a determined wave rolling up a seashore. Along with the relief came some hope, maybe not a lot of hope, but hope nevertheless.

His thoughts drifted to their high school years together. Once Meredith's parents gave their reluctant approval, the teens started dating every weekend. His dad would usually drive them, and as the season warmed they could take his scooter sometimes. By the time late spring arrived, Mr. and Mrs. Gold had decided that Clint was a nice young fellow who was always polite to them and treated their daughter with respect. Gradually they let go of their need to have Meredith date only Jewish boys, especially as they saw that she was only going to date Clint and had no interest in any other boys, regardless of their religion.

When summer vacation arrived for the teens, Clint looked for a temporary job. He wanted to save enough money to buy a car so they could enjoy it together. She would be spending the summer working at her parents Pharmacy and she asked them if they would consider hiring her boyfriend for the summer. They jumped at the chance. Many years later they told him it was because they thought that if the two teens worked together all summer it would either split them apart or confirm their dedication to each other.

That was a wonderful summer for Clint. He loved every moment of being anywhere near Meredith, and he actually liked Mr. and Mrs. Gold. Working in the Pharmacy wasn't physically demanding, like many of the summer jobs were around the farming community, so he felt grateful about that also. Life was good for Clint. He began saving money to buy a car.

Up until then, he and Meredith had only brief times alone with each other. They always kissed and hugged whenever they could, but limited opportunity usually kept him from trying to progress further. Once he had a car, he planned, they could have hours at a time together.

Wilma headed off to her Bible study and potluck at the church, leaving Clint behind in his forest clearing. She felt lighter and happier than she had in many years. *It's so wonderful! He's finally come to his senses. Now he'll be fine. I hope he'll clean himself up, too. Oh, how wonderful. My Clint finally taking care of himself! I know he'll recover in Roanoke and be back to his old self in no time. Then maybe he and I ... wait a minute. Whatever am I thinking? I'm married. And he's still married to Meredith. Maybe he'll finally get over his pain, but I'm still married. What I need to do is help him. That's all, just help him. I'm married.*

In those moments, she wasn't even worrying about what he was going to say to Rocky later that morning. Somehow or other she would deal with that, but getting Clint fixed up was the most important thing to her now. Soon she would have to think up reasons to get her husband to let her go to Roanoke so she could secretly visit him in the hospital, but she'd have time to figure that out later. It was a good day, indeed.

For the first time in decades, Clint actually felt pleasure as he remembered something of his time with Meredith. It was a feeling he had long since forgotten. And now here it was – pleasure. Almost a foreign concept to the chronically sad old man, but here it was anyway. Sitting there waiting for Gus to return to the gas station, he began to remember one of his milestone dates with Meredith. As it slowly materialized into his mind, he was for the first time reliving some of the pleasure he had felt those many, many years ago when it had actually happened.

It was during the summer of 1946, before he bought his first car. They had a date to go bowling one warm Saturday night after they both got off work at the Pharmacy, and he arrived on his scooter. When she opened the door after his knock she immediately said, "My parents are out for the evening".

His thoughts raced ahead to what that could mean for them this evening, and why did she tell him before he even greeted her? Was she ready to do more than kiss? And how much more? Or maybe she was just informing him, and still planned to go bowling? He didn't know what to do so he just sort of froze. That didn't deter the young woman, who promptly wrapped her arms up around his neck and started kissing him, gently touching his lips with her tongue just the way he liked. She was pressed tightly against him, and the combination of her tongue and her closeness was driving him crazy with desire for her.

He knew she was a touching kind of person, as he had frequently seen her touch so many of the boys at school, although she stopped doing that after their first date together. And she touched her girl friends and frequently hugged her parents. So when she would touch him it could easily have been just the way she was and not particularly meaningful. But to him a touch from Meredith, no matter how slight or brief, was like a touch from an angel in heaven.

When they slow danced together she always came fully up against him, warmly, and feeling so compliant in his arms; when that happened he could barely contain himself as emotions would invariably sweep over him from head to toe. Yet he sensed that if she were to slow dance with someone else, she wouldn't hug in closely at all. That thought always made him feel as if he were very special to her. And when she did press up against him, so wonderfully, he invariably rose firmly to the occasion. Yet she didn't try to back away from his pelvic area at all. It confused him no end how she could be so intimate in the one sense, but would not allow him any other touching of her private areas.

This time, she was fully against him while teasing his lips with her tongue. By the time she pulled away, he was breathing hard with his heart racing furiously. He feebly asked, "Can we stay here instead of going bowling?"

"Are you sure you wouldn't rather go bowling?" she asked in her teasing tone. "We might not find anything to do if we just stay here, and I certainly wouldn't want you to be bored." She lightly brushed her fingertips across his lips and continued, "After all, you might get tired of me if you get bored. And then I wouldn't have a steady date anymore." With that pronouncement, she turned and ran into the house, laughing the whole way.

"Oh, it's you," she said, nonchalantly, after he had come in speechlessly and closed the door. "I wondered if you were coming in". Then she laughed again and told him, "Start the fireplace while I put on some music. It'll be real romantic."

He still couldn't really say much of anything, but did as he had been told. There was already wood and kindling in the fireplace. Even though the weather had turned warm, he knew the Gold's kept the fireplace ready in case they wanted to relax and read during the evening. He lit the kindling and adjusted the screen, then turned off the lights even though she hadn't said to do that. The fire's glow grew rapidly to a full flame and lit the room romantically. She had the record player going now, with soft, easy songs. She waited for him, standing beside the table that held the record player, with a mischievous look on her lovely face.

He knew she liked to dance with him, and he always loved to have her press up against him, so he quickly took her in his arms and they started slow dancing. She rested her head on his shoulder and he whispered "I love you" to her.

It had only been very recently that he had dared say those words, because he had been afraid they might scare her away. But that hadn't happened, although she had yet to say them back. He hoped she would then, in that romantic and private setting, but she didn't.

Oh well, at least she seems to like it when I say it to her. Someday she'll love me too. Or at least I sure hope so. Meanwhile I've got the greatest girl ever in my arms and she at least likes me a whole lot.

After a couple of dances they adjourned to the kitchen for a snack, then when they returned to the living room the light from the fireplace made everything so romantic and inviting that he took her hand and led her over to the sofa facing the fire. He sat down and pulled her down next to him. She sat close, but he scooted even closer and put his right arm around her and began gently kissing her. He had experimented with different types of kissing, and knew she didn't like sloppy or harsh ones. Being a patient fellow, he could administer gentle kisses quite well and didn't have a need to be forceful about it.

After a while he began kissing the rest of her face, her eyes and her cheeks. She whispered, "Oh darling, I'm so happy here with just the two of us. This is wonderful. Don't stop kissing me, I love it so much."

Any thought of stopping had certainly not crossed his mind, even without the encouragement. But she had never before said anything to him when they were kissing, so this was momentous. His heart surged in his chest and he felt even more love for this wondrous girl in his arms.

He gently and lightly pressed his tongue into her warm mouth and she received it lovingly, slowly caressing his tongue with her own. He could feel his heart pounding and his emotions rising. With his body touching hers so closely, he could feel her heart racing, and her warmth was intoxicating. She was turned towards him and he reached around her and slowly stroked his left hand up and down her back, then kissed her neck, knowing how much she loved it when he did those things together. Kissing and nibbling gently, he heard her just begin to moan ever so quietly with pleasure.

He longed to have more of her, all of her. His longing grew stronger and stronger, driven by her quiet moaning, by her loving embrace, and by her warmth and openness to him. She had never before moaned like that when they were kissing. He shifted his legs to relieve the painfully tight pressure of his pants on his groin, but to no avail. He was too intensely erect and every time she moaned he seemed to grow even more. The pain had become strong enough to get his attention, but he knew if he broke their entanglement to adjust everything it would be difficult to return to such an intense moment together. He resolved to ignore the pain, no matter what.

They sat intertwined, with her right arm and hand across them and wrapped around his shoulder. Slowly, carefully, he began to move his left hand along her right arm and shoulder, then slightly down her shoulder blade and just barely into her armpit. With his heart racing, he held there for a moment, waiting to see if his hand would be pushed away as she had always done before. Waiting. And waiting. It seemed an eternity. Did she know what he was planning? Did she feel his hand so close to her breast? He nibbled on her left earlobe and she moaned softly. He moved his hand slightly and felt the heel of his hand against the side of her firm breast. Oh, the agony and the ecstasy of the moment.

He waited again. And again she moaned softly. His pants were getting damp. He moved his hand until he could feel the side of her breast, and nibbled her earlobe again. Slowly the realization came to him that she wasn't going to stop him, that finally after weeks and weeks of dating he was actually going to hold her breast in his hand. With that realization his pants got even damper, but he barely noticed. Instead, he moved his hand slowly around the rest of the way and found heaven.

Gently he squeezed the only breast he had ever held. He continued kissing and nibbling her neck. Gently and softly she moaned. His own moan started deep in his throat and grew rapidly into a yell as he ejaculated into his pants. He held her breast the whole time, and Meredith, knowing what was happening, held him closely until his shaking had stopped. He went to the bathroom to clean up his mess, and by the time he returned her parents were pulling up in their car. As he was leaving and saying goodbye to her, he saw the deepest love in her eyes that he had ever seen.

NINE

The preacher may not have been in his finest form that Wednesday morning, or perhaps it was just Wilma's inability to concentrate. Whatever the reason, she didn't hear most of what he said, and he seemed to be going on forever that morning. The subject matter didn't interest her that much anyway; she felt that she was already spiritual, and came to these meetings for the potluck and socializing rather than for any higher religious training. Not that the bible study at her church could ever be considered higher learning, but it was sometimes interesting. Today, though, she didn't think she would even enjoy the socializing after the lesson. After all, the man she had worried about for so many years had finally come to his senses. Perhaps, though, she ought to pray that it wasn't too late for his treatments to work. As if on cue, right then the preacher said his "let us pray" and she promptly started beseeching God to get Clint healed up.

As soon as bible study ended she rushed to the ladies room, the one that was out of the way and rarely ever used, and sat inside with tears running down her face. Soon she was sobbing. At first she tried to stop, but it all just kept coming. *Why am I crying so? I should be happy, not blubbering like a baby. Is it because he's finally going for help? It's about time he wised up. I pray he didn't wait too long. However will I get down to Roanoke? I need to go see him several times a week. How can I do that? Abe's suspicious anyway and he'll never believe any old story I come up with. But I just have to go. Supporting Clint to get better is so important. Or am I crying because of Rocky? He'll be asking tough questions after Clint talks to him. What do I tell him? It's his past, too, so I have to be truthful. He'll probably hate me. And what about Abe? I haven't been happy with him for so long. Am I crying because of him? Maybe because I'm married to him? Maybe I'm crying about all of that. Oh dear God, please help me through this and help Rocky to not hate me. And please help dear Clint get better.* Finally, after what seemed a long time, she stopped crying.

Just thinking about Abe and her marriage made her nervous and anxious. It seemed as if his drinking had been getting worse, or perhaps it was just that her tolerance for it was decreasing. At any rate, she didn't like to think too much about it. She had no job skills and if she ever left him she'd be unable to support herself. And that wasn't even considering her son, who still needed to finish high school and then, she fervently hoped, go on to college somehow. Although the money for college wasn't going to be a problem now, if Rocky would be willing to accept it. But even so, that wasn't going to do her own situation any good.

Wilma washed her face and quickly reapplied her makeup, dreading that she would have to go face all those people after having disappeared from the group. *I'll have to think of something to say. But I'm afraid no one will believe any excuse I might come up with. Well darn it. Might as well go get through this thing.*

------- <<>> -------

Still sitting at Gus's, Clint was actually feeling fond memories of that momentous Saturday night date when he had first touched her breast. All of a sudden he realized he was feeling good thinking about it. For the usually sad man this came as a shocking revelation. Was he dishonoring Meredith by feeling happiness instead of sadness? He wasn't quite sure, but he knew one thing - the happiness felt wonderful.

He even chuckled to himself when he remembered that after leaving her house that evening he had been so distracted he walked half way home before remembering his motor scooter was still at her house. And it was a painful walk at that, with the insides of his underwear and pants sticky. His privates and the insides of his upper thighs were chapped and sore for days afterwards. But holding her breast had been totally worth it.

In his entire lifetime, that date was one of the events he always remembered as being a watershed moment in his youth. Before Meredith went away years later, whenever he thought back on it he always had very fond feelings associated with the whole event, even the chapped, sore and very tender aftermath. Now, today, feeling some of that fondness was like old times, happier times. So he continued, going through his memory of what had happened the next time he talked with her.

"Oh don't be silly," Meredith had said. "You shouldn't be embarrassed around me. I understand how boys are. Besides, it makes me feel special that you get so excited when you're with me. So stop being silly."

She took another bite of her sandwich, as if the whole matter was now put to rest.

"But, I ..." he stammered, still embarrassed. He had just apologized for his behavior at her house the previous Saturday night, and was completely surprised at her attitude about the whole thing.

"I like it when you touch me and Saturday the touching was really special. And I like it when it excites you. I told you it makes me feel special to you. And I really do know about how boys are. So knock it off. Will you share that cookie with me?"

He handed her the cookie, being no longer interested in eating. What he had just heard from her was going to take some thinking on his part before he could fully absorb what it all meant. But one thing really troubled him in what she had just said. He knew she had dated some boys in their school, and he assumed that before she moved from Atlanta she had dated city boys there. She had a knack for wrapping hapless boys around her little finger, practically without trying. So surely she had lots of experience with boys. Adding to the mystery, she was very protective of herself physically with him and had only just allowed him to touch her breast.

What bothered him was, just how did she know those things about boys? And how did she understand that he had ejaculated in his pants while he held her breast, and while she had continued to hold him close the whole time? He thought he knew her well enough to be pretty sure that she was a virgin, yet she could and sometimes did completely surprise him in a way that made him wonder. He couldn't just ask her directly, but the whole thing bothered him a great deal.

Finally, after pondering all of those troubling thoughts for a few minutes, he lost his self-control and blurted out, "How do you know such things about boys, anyway?"

"So, you are jealous after all. And all of this time I thought you weren't. Well, buster, I should have known it. Guess you're just like those other guys. I'm so disappointed."

He was aghast. How had he been so stupid and now maybe ruined everything he had worked so long and hard to accomplish? His heart sank all the way to his feet and he felt like crying. Then he saw it, but in the midst of his despair it took some moments to sink in. That mischievous look in her eyes and the way she kept a steady gaze right on him, watching and waiting. He knew her well enough to know what that meant, but it still took a bit for him to realize that he wasn't in as much trouble as he had thought. Finally, he said, "Well, maybe I'm a little jealous. But I would like to know, if you'd be willing to tell me," he said, thankful that he had figured out something intelligent to say that would hopefully not get him in any deeper.

"I'll tell you anything you want to know. I don't have any secrets from you. Remember I've told you how I used to spend the summers on my uncle's farm before we moved up here from Atlanta?"

Just then Mrs. Gold called them back to work from sitting on the back steps behind the Pharmacy. Clint immediately started trying to figure out how he could bring up the subject again later so he could relieve his very troubling anxiety. As much as he loved her, he sometimes longed for those days back before he had ever seen her, when his life had been much simpler and he didn't have to always be trying to figure out the opposite sex.

A bit later, standing around in the social hall, two or three of Wilma's friends asked where had she been, and was anything wrong. She of course said everything was just fine. But she certainly was worried about everything, especially what Clint would be saying to Rocky that very day. She couldn't get past the worry, knowing her son would come home with plenty of anger and upset, and she had better prepare herself to deal with it. Maybe she'd better say a lot of prayers about that all working out, she thought to herself.

After what seemed an eternity it was over. The preacher had gone on and on that morning, then the lunch was late because no one had remembered to warm the oven ahead of time, and everyone seemed to want to talk and talk. Finally, later than usual, she was just starting to drive away from church. She thought perhaps she should drive to town and see if Rocky, Clint and Teaser were meeting yet. But no, she thought, it'll be better to leave Rocky alone until he's ready to talk. She knew her son to be thoughtful and intelligent, and not given to flying off the handle like Abe, and he would come to her soon enough with his questions and feelings. Or perhaps it was just her fear of facing up to it all, and maybe she should approach Rocky herself? Well, she wouldn't have an opportunity to do that anyway, so the reason for procrastinating didn't really matter. Either way, approaching Rocky or not doing so, it surely would be difficult to deal with.

Most of all, she hoped he would be patient enough to understand her side of it and not just hate her. She didn't know how she could live if her only child hated her.

Just as she pulled up at home, her whole body started shaking and she felt faint, but managed to get the car stopped. She felt so nervous about the whole thing that she barely managed to stagger into the house. The shaking kept up, and now she began feeling nauseous. After a bit her body calmed down some. Thankfully, with Abe working day shift that week, he wasn't home so at least she wouldn't have to deal with any of his stuff.

The minutes were ticking by ever so slowly, and she kept nervously looking out the window every few moments wondering when Rocky would be coming home. Then she remembered about Clint's trunk full of photo albums and Meredith's diaries. She knew she'd better get it out of the car right away and hide it somewhere, before anybody else got home, no matter how nauseous or shaky she might still be feeling. The trunk was heavy for her, so by the time she got it down to the basement she had to rest a few moments before hiding it away. She felt funny thinking about the possibility of reading someone's intimate diary, especially since they were penned by the wife of the man she longed for. *Perhaps just a quick peek. He said I should do it. Maybe just one short passage. Just enough to know a little tiny bit about who she was.*

Clint had dozed off. The ancient wooden chairs had clearly not been designed for comfort, as everyone pointed out to Gus whenever they sat in one of them. But they provided the forum some of the old men in town needed to get together and tell stories and lies to each other. In fact, the universal awareness that the chairs were so uncomfortable made them a readily available topic of conversation for the men, since it was frequently the case that they couldn't think of any other way to start up an interchange with each other. As for Gus, who was apparently very wise in the ways of male bonding, he steadfastly refused to replace them and instead kept repairing them despite their age.

Over the years Clint had spent many, many hours in that very chair, and had, regardless of its quality, returned readily to it almost daily for a decade or more. So it was no surprise that he fell sound asleep even while sitting atop something akin to a torture machine for the back and butt. But, sadly, the fact is that he felt so much pain in other areas of his body that the chair was no longer much of an irritant. He wouldn't stay asleep for more than a few minutes at a time, anyway, then as he always did he would stand and pace back and forth a couple of times before retaking his seat.

Something was different this time when he awoke and stood up to pace a bit. At first he couldn't put his finger on it, but something in the way he was feeling seemed out of place. Then he was startled to realize that he was feeling peaceful and perhaps even a bit happy. Long ago such feelings were his norm, but after so many years of inner struggle it heralded a momentous change of events. He even smiled to himself, thinking that maybe, just maybe, life might someday be good again.

Wilma looked in the old trunk and decided on a particular diary. They were of different sizes and colors, some with fabric covers that were now faded to blandness. Some had leather covers, and some just pressboard. But she knew each of them came from a person that Clint idolized, so she would treat them respectfully. She closed the trunk lid and sat down on it, feeling nervous at what she was about to do.

"Dear diary" it started off on the page that had been opened at random. She noticed that Meredith had a fluid, smooth, and inviting penmanship style. Wilma closed the book without reading another word, feeling as if she were violating Meredith and Clint both. But he had said Meredith would feel honored to have her memory shared with someone that was so special to him, so she opened the book again and began to read.

"Sept. 9, 1946. Dear diary, I saw Clint before homeroom today and he said he almost had enough saved up. He was so excited and he's so cute when he's like that. He's been wanting that blue car that's for sale over at the gas station. He showed it to me last Saturday. He said it's beautiful. I guess it's a boy thing – to me it looked like an old car. But of course I didn't tell him that."

"I can hardly wait for him to get it. Then he can drive up to my house and pick me up in his very own car! It'll be such fun – he said he would take me to school every day. I can sit right next to him while we're driving along. Maybe he'll kiss me whenever we stop at the red lights. He's gotten to be such a good kisser. At first I wasn't sure he would ever learn how. I'm almost certain I'm his first and only kiss."

"I remember that first kiss. Our first real kiss, that is. It was on my front porch and I had to do it to him because I don't think he would have ever gotten up his nerve. I had to find out if he liked me or not. I was pretty sure he did, but I couldn't keep waiting forever to be sure. I stood there looking up into his cute face with his big blue eyes so I just did it – I put my arms up around his neck and did it. He seemed kind of awkward, but he put his arms around me and it felt wonderful. When our lips touched together it felt even more wonderful. It never felt like that with any of the other boys I've kissed."

"I felt warm all over, with his arms around me and mine stretched up around his neck. We were real close together and I could feel him holding me tight. I'm so happy that he likes me. And I'm really happy that he's gotten to be a better kisser too!

"As soon as I went inside I peeked out the curtain beside the door and I saw him fall down the steps. I wanted to run outside to see if he was hurt but if I did then he'd know I'd been watching him, but if I didn't he might just lie there injured and alone. Thank G-d he got up and looked OK, then he tripped again while walking away. That kiss must have really gotten to him. It was then that I knew for sure he liked me."

She closed the diary and recalled her own first real kiss and how romantic she had thought it was going to be, but then how awkward it actually turned out. After reading Meredith's diary, even just that one entry, she was already feeling some empathy for the girl. Up until then, Meredith had been just a person that Clint pined after, a person that had died 39 years ago. Now the 16-year-old had a voice of her own. She decided to read more as soon as she could.

She kept the diary out and carefully covered Clint's trunk with some old boxes to hide it. The diary could stay under her mattress. Since Abe never made the bed he wouldn't find it there. When she took it up to her bedroom she was thinking how close and intimate that might make the two women, with the one sleeping just inches away from the other's personal and intimate writings. For some reason, that felt very comforting to her.

TEN

A motorcycle roared by on the street in front of the gas station. The loud rumble from the open pipes startled Clint and brought him back into the moment. As much as he loved Teaser, whenever he heard a motorcycle that was way too loud he cringed. After all, other people didn't like to be disturbed and it just gave all motorcyclists a bad name.

He had a momentary troubling thought, but promptly put it out of his mind, just as he always did when that particular subject crept in unexpectedly. But then he reconsidered, knowing that the moment of truth was approaching rapidly and he'd better figure it out now, not while face-to-face with Rocky. He knew the boy was smart, but he didn't have any idea what type of questions he might ask.

The impending conversation with Rocky had been troubling him for many years, and he had put it off time and time again. *But I don't know if I'll ever be back from Roanoke so I can't put it off any longer. I need to do my duty and just deal with it. But how? That's the question. And just how much should I actually tell him? Everything? Or as little as possible? There's just no easy way out of it. No wonder I've put it off so long.*

------- <<>> -------

She kept looking toward her bedroom. Just sitting in the living room, waiting for Rocky to come home, was becoming unbearable. Finally, Wilma couldn't stand it another moment and walked quickly into the bedroom and retrieved Meredith's diary from under the mattress. She held the book in her hands and even held it against her heart, all the while thinking how interesting that in having read only one brief passage she was already feeling a special bond with the young girl that had so long ago written about her life and emotions.

After treasuring the diary for a time, she leafed through a few pages until she came upon one that felt, somehow, to be inviting her to come in and share the experience.

"August 2, 1946. Dear Diary, what a wonderful day it's been! I'm almost too tired to write to you tonight, but I just have to. Mom and Dad let us both have the day off today so we could go for a picnic lunch together. Clint picked me up on his scooter this morning and we rode as far as we could toward Old Maid's Creek then parked the scooter at the end of the dirt road where the trail starts. There were only two cars there, so we knew there wouldn't be very many people at the creek or lake, which meant we could find a private spot for our picnic.

"As soon as we got our backpacks and started up the trail, he grabbed my arm and stopped me in my tracks. At first I didn't know what was going on, but then he pulled me up to him and started kissing my forehead, then my eyes, then my cheek. When he got to my ear I practically fainted right there in his arms! He must have felt me getting weak all over but he didn't stop – when he started kissing the side of my neck it was just so wonderful and romantic that I started mewing. I'm sure he must have heard me even though I tried to keep it quiet. I could barely stand up but his arms felt so strong around me.

"I've always really liked being kissed by him, but this time it was different. My whole body tingled and felt warm all over! It was a strange feeling that I haven't had before, but I sure liked it. I pulled even closer with my arms around him and it was fantastic just feeling him all pressed against me from head to toe. Then, and Dear Diary you just have to keep this a <u>secret</u>, when we started walking again I realized that my panties were damp! That's never happened to me before and it completely befuddled me. He must have thought I was acting crazy because I couldn't even keep a conversation going!

"Oh Diary, what's happening to me? I've always been completely in charge around boys. It's always me that befuddles them and I've loved that. They always fall apart when I pay attention to them. Now it's me that fell apart. What's happening to me?

"Thank goodness he didn't stop to kiss anymore along the way because I was just so beside myself I wouldn't have known what to do! He liked for me to walk in front on the narrow parts of the trail and I could feel his eyes on me, but I didn't mind at all. Then one time just for fun I made him go in front and he was so nervous he kept almost tripping on the rocks. But it gave me a chance to look at him and that was fun too. He's such a cute klutz whenever I surprise him in a way that embarrasses him.

"What a beautiful day with the blue sky and a few white puffy clouds and warm air. And being with my boy friend, too. We got to Old Maid's Creek then took the trail beside the creek to the lake. We passed two couples and went further around to a lovely spot with a meadow that started at the edge of the lake and went to the edge of the forest. We put out our blanket at the edge of the meadow where we were shaded by the big trees. What a romantic spot, with the meadow and the lake and the trees and Clint.

"We both lay on our backs and watched the clouds. We had such fun looking for shapes in the clouds and making up stories about where they were going and what they were going to do. Lying on the blanket next to him kept me feeling warm and loved. It's so much fun doing things with just the two of us. Then after awhile I started wondering if he was going to kiss me lying there. We had never kissed while lying down, and I was really wishing he would hurry up and get to it. I couldn't figure out why he would just let that opportunity pass by. Boys! He's always trying to touch me, but where is he when I want to be touched?

"I kept thinking I would have to start it myself if he wasn't going to. The feelings in my body from our kiss on the hiking trail were still warm and exciting and I wanted him to kiss me immediately. Finally I think he must have read my mind because he moved over so our sides were touching real close and he held my hand. No kiss yet, but at least he was making progress. So I reached over with my other hand and stroked his arm. I could feel the change in him – he always seems to melt when I stroke him. I remember thinking that now if that doesn't get him to make a move I don't know what will.

"At last! So he was still alive after all. He turned on his side and started kissing me and it was fantastic. I turned toward him and we were touching and he French kissed me and I mewed again. He must have heard my mewing and known I was so happy and open to him, because he started kind of gently wriggling against me as he held me all over. My whole body got real warm and tingly again and that thing happened to my panties again (remember Diary you're keeping this a secret). We kissed and held each other a really long time before we both needed to rest from it. My dearest Diary, it was the absolutely most breathtaking and wonderful experience I've ever had!

"We decided to swim before lunch so we each hid behind some trees and changed into our swimsuits and then had so much fun playing and splashing in the water. It was the first time he had ever seen me in a swimsuit and he couldn't keep his eyes off me. He tried to hide it and not be real obvious, but the poor guy was pretty much a goner and couldn't look at anything else. Not that I minded, even though I couldn't let him know that. In fact, it makes me feel really good when he can't seem to concentrate on anything else when I'm there. But now it's the strangest thing, because sometimes I can't concentrate when he's there.

"After lunch we played cards until he couldn't stand losing anymore. I didn't tell him I used to play poker with the boys and men at my uncle's farm during the summers and that they had taught me all about bluffing and how to lead your opponent into thinking they had a better hand. Some of my girlfriends say they always let their boyfriends win at cards and bowling, but for sure that's not me. Poor Clint, he didn't stand a chance. So I decided to make it up to him ...

"As soon as he put the cards away in his backpack I came up behind him and hugged him tightly and told him thank you for being such a good sport at cards. I held him for a long time and kissed him on his back. Afterwards he was in a real good mood again. Then we decided on another swim and raced to the water, but he's a fast runner and beat me. I think he needed to do that. You know, that macho boy stuff.

"This time we both actually swam instead of just splashing and hugging. We can both swim a little and it was fun to practice getting better together. We swam to the other side of the lake and from there could see that there were more people around the lake, but still no one near our spot.

"After our swim he got to the towels first and wouldn't give me one. I held out my hand and told him to give it to me right now. He had a mischievous smile and I knew it would take more than just telling him. Then he asked me if he could dry me off and I told him not even in his dreams and that he'd better shape up right now. He just stood there, still smiling. I started thinking that he had already touched me in lots of places, so what would it matter if he dried me off? Besides, it would be fun to have my boy friend dry me off all over. It would certainly be a new adventure. So what harm could there be, I thought. He must have sensed that I was softening because then he said I dare you to let me do it. Dear Diary, you know I almost never pass on a dare, so I said all right, buster boy, you can do it. But if you don't behave they'll never find your dead body at the bottom of the lake.

"Oh, Dear Diary, it was awesome. He was so gentle and loving while he rubbed the towel all over me. He had such a look of joy on his face the whole time, especially when he dried my breasts and butt. Then he was so awkward when he went to dry between my legs, but I just stood my ground and glared at him even though I loved the whole thing. He was breathing hard by the time he finished. I just love it when I excite him so much without doing anything at all.

"We sat down and he kissed me again, then he moved me so we were lying down beside each other and he rolled so he was just a little bit on top of me and kissed my ears and neck. It was so wonderful I started mewing again. Our legs were rubbing against each other and since we still had on our swimsuits it felt so grownup with his bare skin against mine and with him part way on top of me.

"Then he whispered I love you in my ear. I didn't know what to do so I just hugged him even tighter. Oh Diary, why did he have to go and say that again? When he says it, it sounds really nice but it also makes me feel really funny. What's wrong with me? I really really like him, but I can't seem to tell him I love him. Do I love him? Is there something wrong with me that I don't even know for sure? It must hurt him that I don't say it back, but I'm just so confused.

"Oh Diary, I'm so tired and sleepy I have to go now. But first I want to tell you the rest of the day was wonderful and I really hated it when he had to bring me home. Good night, Dear Diary."

Wilma carefully put the diary safely back under her mattress and then sat on the side of the bed. She felt envious of the young girl because she herself had never had such romantic experiences as a teen. Or ever, for that matter. Meredith was one lucky girl, she thought, to have had such a wonderful young life with a boy as special as Clint. As Wilma sat there, she suddenly realized why she was feeling out of breath with tightness in her chest and an ache in her groin – to her utter astonishment she had become quite aroused while reading the diary. How amazing, she thought, getting aroused reading about Meredith. Then the truth hit her. It wasn't Meredith's experience that had aroused her; it was the idea of being with Clint.

She lay back on the bed and started rubbing herself. At first she felt guilty, but didn't know why. It had been years since Abe had satisfied her in bed, so she had made masturbation a normal part of her life. And she often thought about Clint at those times. So why would she feel guilty now, she wondered? Well, guilty or not, she wasn't turning back. Then all thoughts drifted away from her mind as she began to feel such a powerful intensity that it was consuming her entire body. Just before the long wailing scream escaped involuntarily from her lips she had a fleeting thought that she had only one time before in her entire life ever had such a powerful and consuming orgasm.

ELEVEN

Enough reminiscing. And enough time sitting in this chair that's probably older than I am. I feel good! Time to get going.

Clint was actually feeling happy as he arose from the uncomfortable wood chair and started toward Teaser. His thoughts and memories about Meredith had been painful for so long that he had practically forgotten what it felt like to be happy, but now he was remembering that he liked it. *Ah, happiness, that's what life with Meredith was all about, and now it's time for that happiness to take me into the next part of my life.*

Teaser started on the first kick, as she always used to back before his sadness and pain had sapped so much of his strength. He pointed her towards Gold's Pharmacy, where her next adventure awaited anxiously. It seemed to take only seconds before the store came into view, then only seconds later and Rocky was there waving at him. He wondered if Rocky would allow him an occasional ride on the old girl after he returned from Roanoke, if he returned at all, that is. "Enough of those negative thoughts," he said aloud just before he pulled up beside the anxious and smiling young man.

"Let's go around back," he said to Rocky, "it'll be more private there."

He drove the motorcycle around behind the Pharmacy and Rocky was somehow standing there practically before the machine came to a halt. As soon as he dismounted, Rocky hugged him and said, "Uncle Clint, I'm so happy that you're here. I brought the money just like you said. I saw you ride out of town. Did you want to take her for a ride before we met?"

"Yes, one last spring morning up into the foothills. I couldn't resist. But we're here now, and there's some things we need to talk about. Let's start with the money and get that out of the way. I told you $182, right?"

"Right. Here it is. I counted it just before you came. It was hard, but I saved it all myself and didn't borrow any of it, just like you said I needed to do."

He took the cash and put it in his pocket without counting it, and handed the ignition key and DMV title papers to Rocky, which he had already filled out and signed. "You'll need to take care of these papers within a few days. You can keep the license plate on her, if you want to. I know she'd like that, and so would I," he said, referring to the personalized license plate that proudly announced TEASER to the world.

"I'd like that too, Uncle Clint." Rocky noticed, curiously, that the license plate was the cleanest thing on the motorcycle.

Clint continued, "You may remember how to start her up and work the controls, but I'd like to review them if that's ok with you."

"Sure". He felt secretly relieved. He remembered everything Clint had ever hold him about Teaser, but a review at this point would help with the anxiety and fear he was feeling. As he looked at Teaser, now that she was his, it surprised him how much bigger she looked. It was, after all, his responsibility now to control her. Uncle Clint had often told him you had to treat her just like a real lady, but that didn't mean anything to Rocky because he had no idea how one should treat a lady. He didn't even have what would be considered real dating experience. His only role model, his father, certainly didn't treat his mom like a lady, either.

Clint discussed every one of the controls with Rocky, having the teen sit on the motorcycle and work the controls as they talked about them. He knew that Rocky had sometimes driven farm machinery around the area, knew how to work a clutch and shift gears, and had his driver's license even though Abe usually didn't allow him to drive the family's car. But on Teaser the clutch is hand operated and the shifter is foot operated, so that would be new to learn. What Clint didn't know was that Rocky had been pretending to ride Teaser for years and had practiced relentlessly on his bicycle, imagining the controls and levers and pedals and working them all the while. Years ago, when Clint had first told Rocky about the various controls, each new bit of knowledge had been incorporated into the bicycle practice sessions while pretending it was Teaser.

"Let's sit on the steps here for a bit. There's something important I want to talk with you about."

Rocky didn't know what could be more important than getting Teaser started and taking off on his first great ride, but he didn't want to be disrespectful so he sat down next to Clint and waited. Besides, he knew the older man well enough to know that this must be really important so he might just as well go along with the wait instead of trying to fight it. Normally it wouldn't be a problem at all, but with Teaser just waiting for him Rocky had a difficult time sitting still. He also felt a bit awkward sitting on the back steps of the Pharmacy because he didn't want anyone to come out and run them off, especially sitting there with Clint who looked like an unkempt bum.

Just then, as if on cue, the door opened and out stepped Mr. Zorn, the Pharmacy's manager. He was a middle-aged man of ample girth, but nevertheless quite energetic. Rocky jumped up and was poised to get away from the porch and steps. Mr. Zorn had a surprised look on his face, which quickly turned to a smile and he said, "Oh, hello Clint. I didn't realize you were back here. And hello to you too, Rocky." Returning his gaze toward Clint, he continued, "Is there anything I can do for you?"

Rocky was startled, to say the least, at Mr. Zorn's attitude toward them and especially since he had directed such a nice smile to Clint. He was even more startled at what happened next.

------- <<>> -------

It had been a tough and very dusty shift. The dust and abrasive grit had worked its way deep into his clothes. His whole body seemed to itch as the stuff rubbed wherever there was a skin crease. He could taste and feel the dirty stuff in his mouth, and he didn't like it one bit. His mood was as foul as his clothes. He knew there were asbestos fibers mixed in with all of it, and that didn't help his disposition. The old thick insulation on the huge steam pipes hadn't come off without a fight, and it had pretty much gotten the better of the whole crew. Days like this happened sometimes, more often than anyone liked. Johnson's Refinery had been originally built many years ago and wasn't designed for ease of maintenance. But getting a shower and clean clothes were far from his mind.

Abe Powlison' taste buds had been getting ready for this moment for hours and they were acutely primed. He could already taste the bitterness of the fermented hops and feel the chill as that first wonderful swallow was just moments from making its way from the bottle to his mouth. He wasn't thinking beyond that first swig because every inch of his body knew just how it was going to feel.

A moment later, the first big slug having been downed, he wasn't disappointed. It had been just as he had imagined. Before even starting on the rest of the bottle he ordered another so there wouldn't be any delay between rounds. He knew, after all, that this would be a long drinking session and he wasn't going to waste a moment of it.

Now, with the first few swallows completed, he started thinking again about what had been bothering him lately. *Wilma's been mouthing off to me lately even more than usual. I'm not gonna keep on taking it from her. And Rocky's even started to pick up some of her attitude. It all has to stop, and I'm gonna make sure it stops soon. No wife and son of mine are gonna back talk me and get away with it. Not now, not ever.*

What's gotten into her, anyway? She's always been a bit uppity, but a few slaps or an occasional punch always shut her up before. Now she's getting to be bitchy most of the time. And she's even started telling me to cut back on my drinking.

No woman's gonna tell me how much I can drink. I'll drink whatever and whenever I damn well feel like it. If she wants me to cut back, then maybe she oughta start acting like a proper wife and stop making me so angry. Then I wouldn't have to drink. So it's her fault, and she keeps making it worse on herself. I'm gonna show her, and soon. This time I won't be so easy on her. Or on Rocky.

The bright daylight startled his eyes a couple of hours later when he staggered out of the bar, squinting. He didn't have a car to drive home in, since he always got a ride to work with one of his buddies on the same shift, and then got a ride to the bar after work. His home was close enough that he could walk from here, and that wasn't usually a problem. But sometimes, like this time, he was so drunk that he passed out before he got home.

Mr. Zorn waited for a reply from Clint. Rocky waited for Mr. Zorn to tell them to get away from the Pharmacy. But Clint didn't wait for anything and replied to Mr. Zorn's question.

"There is one thing you could do for us, Victor. Would you please tell everyone to not use the back door for a while? Young Rocky and I are having a private discussion and don't want to be disturbed."

To Rocky's amazement Mr. Zorn immediately agreed and then retreated back into the store. "Uncle Clint," Rocky asked while sitting back down, "why didn't Mr. Zorn chase us away? And why did he do what you told him to do?"

"Rocky, my boy, that's one of the things I want to tell you about. You see, I own the Pharmacy. Victor has managed it for me a long time now. I've owned it since Mr. and Mrs. Gold passed away many years ago. They left it to me because their only child had been my wife and they knew how much she loved me. And they loved me too, as the son they had never had."

Rocky hadn't a clue that Clint was the Pharmacy's owner. He had just assumed it belonged to Mr. Zorn. That explained how Clint got enough money to buy food, but it didn't explain why he lived as a homeless person. Rocky was about to ask him about that when the man started speaking again and answered the unasked question.

"I know I look and act like a hobo or some kind of bum, but that's going to change." He paused for a moment, then continued, "I've been feeling very poorly since Meredith died. You know she was my wife many years ago, right?" Without waiting for a reply, he said, "She was wonderful and I've missed her every day since she died. Then I got sick with this cancer and felt even worse."

"Did you know about the cancer, Rocky?" he quietly asked.

"Mom told me. I went to the library and read up on it. I've been really worried about you, Uncle Clint. I wish you would go to the doctor and get well. I want my old Uncle Clint back again." His eyes teared up while he was speaking and then he hugged Clint. He was glad they were out of sight because he wouldn't want to be seen acting like a girl, but his emotions were more powerful than he had realized, and then he started crying.

"I didn't know you felt that way about me, my boy. I've really missed you too, more than you know. Now I realize that there are two people in this world that love me and that's a really special thing." Clint held him until Rocky sat up and mumbled something about blubbering like a girl, to which Clint gently and lovingly replied, "It's just us two men here and no one else saw you."

"Well," Clint continued after a bit, "you'll be happy to know I've arranged to get treatment and I'm going to Roanoke to a specialized hospital. I'll be there for several months, I imagine."

Victor Zorn peeked out through the blinds on the door's window. He rarely ever saw Clint and it had been quite a shock to find him on the back porch. He knew Clint came into the store sometimes at night because in the morning there would be a list of the cash and items that had been taken from the safe and store shelves.

He felt sorry for the old man, knowing that he had cancer and evidently not being able to function very well. But there wasn't anything he could do for Clint, as it had been made very clear many years ago that Clint wanted to be left alone.

How nice it would be if Clint was coming out of his shell some and would start to take better care of himself. He didn't want him around the store looking like a beggar, but if he would clean himself up then it would be ok. Not that he himself could stop Clint from looking how he chose or hanging out wherever it suited him, but Mr. Zorn took his job seriously and wouldn't want anything to interfere with the good reputation of the Pharmacy. Even if that interference came from the owner himself.

Mr. Zorn had been the assistant manager when Clint stopped going in to the store many years before, and then he excelled as the manager. Gold's Pharmacy and its reputation for integrity and customer service was his passion. The store thrived under his stern but compassionate leadership. So it was curiosity tinged with considerable concern that drove him to spy on the store's reclusive owner and the teenager.

It was very strange that Clint was sitting there with a youngster. He knew Rocky, as he knew practically everyone in the whole area, but he couldn't imagine what the two of them might have in common. What on earth could they be talking about? Then his discretion came into focus and he quickly walked away from the door, somewhat ashamed of himself. It was none of his business and that's the only thing he really needed to know.

TWELVE

"The cancer took away what happiness was left in me. I went off to die in the woods, alone, but somehow that didn't happen and I'm still here."

Clint stopped speaking. Rocky was still taking it all in. Now some of the pieces of the past were being put into order. Hearing that Clint was still sad about his dead wife and then getting cancer gave some insight into how he had become an unkempt shadow of himself.

"What happened to Meredith, Uncle Clint?"

"We were married for 12 years and I loved every minute of it. But she left me in 1960, before you were born. It was the saddest day of my life. I wish I had it to do over, maybe I could have changed something and it wouldn't have happened."

"Where did she go?"

"After we finished college both of us worked at her parent's Pharmacy. I was the Pharmacist and pretty soon she moved up to be the store manager. She really wanted to expand the business and kept adding new merchandise. Back in those days small town pharmacies weren't like today where drug stores sell everything you can think of. Gold's Pharmacy just had medicines and home remedies. But things changed pretty quick once Meredith started in on it.

"First she added some veterinary supplies and medicines. Her parents were against it, but she always had a way about her and it didn't take her long before they gave in. Well, those animal products sure sold well. So when she started adding other merchandise her parents pretty much stayed out of her way. Before long the Pharmacy had doubled its income.

"Meredith wanted to go to a big trade conference in Baltimore. Her father usually went, but he wasn't feeling well that year. Her parents were so happy with the way she ran the store that they agreed. She got her train tickets and hotel reservations all setup. For her, it was one of the most exciting things she had ever done. We had never spent a night apart since getting married, but I gave her my full blessing to go because it was so important to her."

Rocky waited, noticing the tears on Clint's cheeks. After a few minutes he asked Clint if he wanted to continue.

"I've gone this far with it, I need to finish now. I want you to know what my life was like and that day was a big part of it. I drove her to the train station in Roanoke early that morning. I didn't let on how hard it was for me to see her go like that, but she acted like a kid in a candy store and I just wanted her to be happy." Clint was crying for real by that time, but he continued on anyway. "That evening the news on the radio said there had been a huge train wreck near Washington."

This time it was Rocky's turn to put his arm around Clint's shoulders. Clint sobbed and sobbed.

Rocky didn't really know what to do or say, but he had once seen his mother comfort a friend of hers whose husband had died, and she had done just what he was doing now. So he continued to sit there with his arm around Clint's shoulders.

------- <<>> -------

The phone startled her. At first she didn't realize where she was, and with the phone demanding attention she didn't have time to figure it out. She noticed that she was on her bed, fully clothed. She knew she had been asleep. And it was daylight outside. It was all very disconcerting.

Wilma answered the phone and it turned out to be Nancy Robertson, a dear friend of hers. She asked if Wilma had time to come over and drive her to the dentist in a little while. Nancy didn't have a car and didn't know how to drive, and would often ask Wilma for a ride when she had an errand to do. If Wilma was busy then Nancy didn't mind taking a taxi, but for both of the women these times were an opportunity to socialize and Nancy was always careful to make sure her requests weren't taking advantage of her friend. Wilma immediately agreed to take her, then hung up the phone. But she didn't leave right away because of still feeling disoriented, and it wasn't time yet for Nancy's appointment.

She sat back on the bed to collect her thoughts. Then she remembered masturbating on the bed. *I must have dozed off after that incredibly amazing orgasm.*

Well now, I deserved a bit of a nap after that one! I'm still feeling flushed. Whew! There's still pressure in my groin. I'll just reach down to enjoy these lingering feelings. Wow! There's another one almost ready! What's come over me? I've never had two in a row by myself before. As her eyes closed and her body tensed she began thinking of Clint and how much she wanted him.

Later, with her mind starting to clear, she straightened the bed covers and left to go get Nancy. On her way out she looked through the house for Rocky but he still wasn't home from his momentous meeting with Clint. She couldn't help worrying about how Rocky would deal with it. He was, after all, going to be hearing things he couldn't have imagined. Lots of things. And she couldn't imagine how she was going to handle it if Rocky became angry with her.

"Did you have any children?" Rocky asked.

Clint's thoughts drifted back to just before he and Meredith were married. He hadn't known much about birth control, and as an inexperienced young man who happened to be in his sexual prime he had been much more interested in the honeymoon rather than in the consequences of the upcoming union.

But Meredith's parents wanted her to get a college education before having children so they took the initiative to sit the young couple down and explain birth control to them. When he realized what her parents were going to talk to them about he turned bright red and kept his face turned down towards his lap. He didn't dare look up. He liked Meredith's parents, and liked their frankness about things, but this was too much. These were her parents, for God's sake, and they just weren't supposed to talk about such things. Besides that, somewhere in his mind he secretly thought that maybe they didn't know how badly he wanted to do their daughter and how he would gladly have given his life for just one time with her.

But obviously they knew their precious girl was soon to be deflowered by the red-faced young fellow sitting in their living room. Clint squirmed.

They kept talking. He kept squirming. Then the old familiar urge to run away rose up in his gut and he almost gave in to it. But his logical side knew better – if he ran from his fiancé's parents they might force their daughter not to marry him and that would be unbearable, so he fought against his urge through the whole embarrassing talk.

He remembered looking out of the corner of his down turned eye to see how Meredith was dealing with the unwelcome topic, and she too had her head drooped down towards her lap. He noticed that her face looked even redder than his, if that were even possible. But her parents were determined, and they periodically asked each of the mortified pair if they understood what they were being told.

So, like it or not, one of the things they learned about was condoms. Then, as if just talking about it weren't enough, a package was produced and a sample came out for show and tell. Clint was aghast, and he could imagine how Meredith must have been feeling.

Later on, right after he and Meredith married, it wasn't a surprise to either of them to be given a supply of condoms before leaving for their honeymoon. Embarrassing, yes. Surprising, no.

In retrospect, he knew it must have been very hard for her parents to have done what they did, but they were always responsible parents to Meredith. He supposed that what they had done was just part of it to them, hard or not.

He realized that Rocky was waiting for him to answer the question. "We tried but Meredith never got pregnant. She had so much love and warmth to give and she wanted children, which was great with me, but it just wasn't to be. We had a very happy life together anyway, but it's too bad she didn't get to pass on her golden attributes."

They sat silently for a time and Rocky tried to remember the pictures of Meredith that he had seen years ago in the Pharmacy, but he could only vaguely recall her.

"So I guess you're still pretty sad, Uncle Clint".

"Rocky, my dear boy, I was up until today. But now that I'm going to get all fixed up in Roanoke at that cancer place I've decided it's time to be happy again. So it's with great happiness that I'm passing Teaser on to you." Clint was coming alive with excitement now, and Rocky started to see the Uncle Clint he remembered from his childhood.

"She's named after Meredith, you know. You see, Meredith just loved to tease me, so I nicknamed her Teaser. Then she bought the motorcycle for me, and sometimes I had trouble getting it started. It was as if the motorcycle were teasing me just like Meredith loved to do. So the name just sort of naturally passed on to the motorcycle. After Meredith was gone it gave me comfort to still have a Teaser in my life. Now she's yours, so a part of Meredith gets to live on with the next generation."

Now Rocky understood why Clint always said Teaser needed to be treated like a lady. It was because of Meredith, who had been his lady, and whom Teaser had been named after. Not only that, but Meredith had even bought the motorcycle for Uncle Clint in the first place! It also explained why Teaser was so important to Clint, but it didn't explain why Clint would be willing to sell her to Rocky. He thought about that for a bit, but decided not to ask about it because he didn't want Clint to change his mind about giving up his special motorcycle.

Clint pulled a piece of paper from his pocket and handed it to Rocky. Then he said, "While I'm thinking about it, here's the address and phone number where I'll be in Roanoke. You call me anytime you want, and please come and visit if you like. They tell me I'll be losing all my hair, but other than that I'll be my same handsome self, except that I'll have on clean clothes for a change!"

Rocky took the paper and pocketed it carefully. He didn't know what to say about all of this new information.

"But that's not the only thing I want to tell you about. You see, I know you're a very smart young man and that you do well in school." Then, in response to the questioning look on Rocky's face, he continued, "That's right, I know how well you do in school. I know a lot about you. You've always been very special to me.

That's why I want you to go to college even though your family can't afford it."

This turn in the conversation startled Rocky, who was still struggling with everything else he had been told. He even forgot about Teaser sitting there waiting for him. He hadn't known that Clint paid any attention to him when he wasn't around. He remembered that Clint had always been especially nice to him at the Pharmacy, and giving him rides on Teaser, but even so this all came as a surprise. And there was even more to come.

"I've already talked with Wilma about it. I'm going to pay for you to go to any college you like. She'll help you with the details about how to get the money. It's important in today's world for a young person to get a college education and I want that for you. So I'm going to pay for it. Whatever it costs, I'll take care of. You just do your studies and get good grades." Clint paused, while Rocky just sat there stunned.

Rocky and his mom had talked about college lots of times, and she had always told him to get good grades and then they would try for a scholarship. He had known that the family couldn't afford to pay his way, and probably couldn't even help out very much, so a scholarship and part-time job were his only hope. Throughout his life his mother had talked to him as if he would be going to college, so he felt as if it was just the natural and normal thing to do. But money would present quite a challenge. So now, with Uncle Clint telling him he could go to any college, Rocky didn't know what to say. The whole conversation with Clint was becoming more and more startling and bizarre.

Clint started talking again, "Oh, and by the way, it's probably best if you don't mention any of this to your dad. He probably wouldn't understand and he might try to stop you from going on to college."

While driving to Nancy's house, Wilma kept marveling at what had transpired in her bedroom. And at her lust towards Clint. Not once in all her years with Abe had she felt that lustful towards her husband. She had loved Clint for years, and often thought about him when her husband was having sex with her, but the overwhelming intensity of the lust she had just experienced was unexpected. And unsettling.

THIRTEEN

"I know this is a lot for you to take in all at once. But there's one more thing. Actually, two more things," Clint said.

"First, just in case you might've been thinking about running away with Teaser, please don't do it. You're young and you need to finish your education before you decide if you really want to run away or not. School first, then run away if you still want to. Teaser will still be there to take you away later on, if that's what you want. Just please don't do it now, for your sake and for mine also."

Clint stood up and paced back and forth between the porch and Teaser a couple of times, trying to figure out how to say the next thing to Rocky. Then, deciding to skip the most difficult part of it, sat down again.

"Now just one more surprise. Then I'll leave you and Teaser alone. I'd really like it if you would consider the possibility of becoming a pharmacist, like I was. This town needs a good pharmacist, someone who knows the people and who's a kind and caring person." After a pause, Clint started again, "And I also just happen to know of a pharmacy that would just love to have you working there some day, after you've finished up college. In fact, I can guarantee you a great job!"

"So there. That's about it. I love you and I'll see you soon." With that, Clint got up, went over to Teaser and started her up, then dismounted and stood a short distance away before Rocky could think of anything to say or ask.

Rocky just sat there for a few moments, feeling overwhelmed at all the things he had just heard. There was so much new information he didn't know where to start at figuring it all out. Then he suddenly realized that Teaser was running, and waiting for him. He got up and tried to clear his head for a moment before mounting her. Once astride the mighty lady, his enthusiasm for the moment returned full force and he twisted the throttle just for the joy of hearing the throaty roar. He was not disappointed.

Inside the store Mr. Zorn sat at his desk near the rear door. When he heard the motorcycle's exhaust roar he had a vague sense that something was different, but he couldn't put his finger on what it might be. At first he ignored the feeling, but then the urge to see what was going on became overpowering. After all, as store manager he needed to know if something were amiss. Or at least that's what he tried to tell himself.

He continued determinedly to work on the paperwork in front of him, but only for a few moments longer. Then he decided that it wouldn't be too nosy if he were to just barely peek out through the blinds to the back porch. He was surprised to see young Rocky on the motorcycle, and Clint nowhere in sight within the field of visibility looking through the blinds. Then when the youngster started riding, somewhat shakily, Mr. Zorn was even more surprised.

He knew how much that motorcycle meant to his boss. Years back when they had worked together in the store Clint would often recount stories about his adventures with Teaser to the employees. Everyone knew what a passion their boss had for the bike, and they enjoyed the stories as Clint always managed to weave laughter into them. So it was quite unexpected to see what he had just witnessed.

Clint hadn't moved and hadn't said anything, while Rocky worked at getting up his nerve to ride for the first time ever as the operator of the beloved Teaser. He had a nagging thought that there must be some more things Uncle Clint needed to tell him about how to ride, but he didn't want to appear foolish to the older man so he didn't say anything. Then his body seemed to go on automatic pilot and his hands and feet did the things they had done so many thousands of times on his bicycle when he used to pretend he was driving Teaser.

With a surge that almost sent him falling off the back of the seat, he was off. Even though he was very much a novice on the motorcycle, he had experience with farm machinery and several times in his mom's car when she had let him drive. Fortunately the area behind the Pharmacy had plenty of open field in front of him and he planned to use most of it. He managed to shakily circle the machine around a bit then he fearfully aimed for the passageway past Uncle Clint and beside the Pharmacy that would take him to the street. That was a mistake, he realized after it was too late to turn aside, because it meant he was going to have to stop.

"WHERE ARE THE BRAKES?" he screamed. "AHHHHHHHH!!!!". The street was coming up way too fast to figure this out. Then he just barely remembered something Uncle Clint had told him numerous times: if you forget which foot presses the rear brake, or which hand is for the front brake, just press both pedals with your feet and squeeze both handles on the handlebars.

He came to an abrupt stop just at the edge of the street. "Thank you, God," he said aloud. Clint appeared at his side and reassuringly rubbed the back of his shoulder, but didn't say anything. Then Rocky set about figuring out what he should have done, and asked Clint for confirmation about how the controls worked. After a brief discussion, he felt confident enough to give it another go.

As for Clint, he wanted to help Rocky, but knew it best to let him learn in his own way. So he didn't say any more than necessary, and didn't chastise Rocky in any way. He just tried to reassure and be loving.

Soon Rocky was on his way again. This time he did better at starting off. He aimed towards his house, with the plan to go past it and on out into the country a ways before turning around.

An hour later he had put some miles on the machine, then managed to somehow maneuver it through his secret path in the woods right to his own back yard. He parked behind the garage and decided to go directly into the house to the bathroom.

There was no one home, so after he finished his business he got a snack and went back out behind the garage and sat on Teaser, thinking about what he would do next.

Clint had been feeling like an old man for a long time. But the spring in his step was more than had been there for many, many years. He thought that he should be sad, having just parted with his beloved Teaser. Or perhaps he should be nervous at the idea of heading off for medical treatment tomorrow. So why, he wondered, was he feeling so happy?

Oh, I know! I just spent more time with Rocky than I have in ages. And I just made him one really happy young fellow. Reasons enough to be happy.

That's not all of it. I'm happy to be letting go of the past and living in the present. Now I know there are people in this world that I love, and I plan to make them a part of my life.

Once back to his shanty, he checked around making sure there was nothing left of any value to him. He would be gone through much of the summer and kids or varmints might make a mess of whatever was there, so he couldn't leave anything that he'd want again. His real valuables were Meredith's diaries and some old photos, and those had already gone to Wilma for safe keeping.

Satisfied that everything had been taken care of, he sat down with candlelight to write a letter for Victor Zorn. He felt it important not just to tell his store manager where he would be for the next few months, but to leave some special instructions. Then, after the Pharmacy had closed for the night, he delivered the letter to Victor's desk and retrieved some cash for his hospital stay. The medical bills would be taken care of by the insurance that the Pharmacy provided for the staff, and his personal needs were simple, but one never knew when some cash might come in handy.

Later, well into nighttime, he laid down to sleep in his old bedraggled blankets. He still felt happy, and looked forward to going to Roanoke the next day. His friend Gus was coming at sunup to take him. *So now, everything's all set. I've got a great adventure planned. I have people to love, a wonderful woman is kind to me, a fine young man likes me, and I'll never sleep in this dump again after tonight. So how about a happy memory before sleep?*

His thoughts didn't take their usual turn back to his time with Meredith. In fact, what came into his mind was a complete surprise. "My God," he said aloud, "I haven't remembered that for a long time. It must've happened about 18 years ago." He closed his eyes and began to actually feel how intense, how wonderful, that experience had been.

He remembered how soft she had felt. How warm. And how she had told him it was ok and that he deserved to feel good. She had been so loving, as if he was the one that had needed comforting that night, not her. His body was becoming aroused just remembering how it had felt to be with her, touching her, inside her. Before long he began stroking himself.

He slept more peacefully that night than he had in years.

Rocky didn't feel ready to take Teaser for another ride. Not just yet. He still needed to recuperate from all the emotions that had been flooding his entire being since he had so shakily maneuvered the iron and steel lady away from Gold's. As he sat there, on the saddle, he felt like a real man. Tall and proud.

He decided to practice starting her up. His parents weren't home, so the noise wouldn't be a problem. And she was warned up and should be easier to start. He set the controls, opened the kick starter lever, and lunged downwards with all his might.

He wasn't a slight or frail lad. Working summers on the farms around town, and doing it part time during the school year, he had a strong body. In fact, some of the girls at school thought him to be cute and occasionally even commented on his nice body. But this lady wasn't impressed.

He tried and tried. After awhile the fatigue and soreness could be felt growing more severe. He must be doing something wrong, but he didn't know what.

The old motorcycle just wouldn't start. It would sputter and even pretend to idle for a brief moment, but it wouldn't take any throttle. Every time he stood on the kick-starter and lunged downward with all his might, it sent ripples of agony through his leg and ankle, and the big V-twin seemed to just chuckle at him. It was as if she were saying, "Ha ha, you twit of a boy; it'll take a real man to stroke me".

After resting and daydreaming for awhile, he tried again. "Treat her like a lady," Uncle Clint had said time and time again. *All right then. How would I treat a lady if I was on top of her, between my legs, and ready to lunge downwards with all my weight? Damned if I know.* But he wasn't to be defeated so easily. He set his mind to it and concentrated as hard as he could, imagining Teaser as a beautiful lady just waiting for him to make her roar.

The huge engine started easily on the very next lunge. And roar she did. He didn't know what he had done differently, but if concentrating on Teaser being a beautiful and willing lady between his legs is what it took, then that's what he was going to do every time.

He was inside the kitchen doing some homework when Wilma got home. It seemed to him that she came inside in a rush and appeared to be anxious to see him, but all she said was something about how are you and I'm here if you want to talk about anything. *That's strange behavior. Does she know I'm befuddled by what Uncle Clint told me today? He said she knows about the college fund. What else does she*

know? Maybe about why he would do such a thing for me? Does she know about Teaser? She visited him this morning. Did he tell her about my motorcycle?

The homework was proving to be more of an exercise in futility than anything else. He couldn't seem to keep his thoughts away from what Uncle Clint had told him, and on having seen her go to his shack in the woods. The significance of college being paid for hadn't fully sunk in, and until he clarified things with her he wouldn't really understand the full impact of it all. Right then was probably the best time to talk with her because his dad wasn't home yet, and Clint had said not to tell him about it. But how to start? Vaguely? Yes, vaguely would be best.

"Mom," he said, "did Uncle Clint talk to you about anything?" That was pretty vague, he thought, congratulating himself on setting it up so she would be the first to tell what she knows.

"Yes he did, dear." She sat down with her son at the table, and waited without saying anything else. He wasn't prepared for that. She was supposed to open up and talk, not sit and wait. He needed for her to say how much she knew before he said anything, but evidently she wasn't going to start first. He didn't know quite what to do because he didn't want to get into trouble about anything, and he was in new territory with her.

Finally he couldn't stand the silence any longer and started talking. "Did he say anything about college?" He thought that would be the safest place to start, since Uncle Clint told him she knew about it. Besides, he didn't know why the offer had been made and she probably did.

"He said he would pay for your college, sweetheart. I think it's just wonderful that he wants to do that for you. You know we can't afford it right now, so this is just wonderful." She was smiling now, and full of energy and happiness at the prospect of her son going to college. "And not just the state college. He wants you to go to the best one you want."

"So it's for real, then?"

"Oh yes. Clint is very trustworthy. He promised it for you, and he'll deliver on it."

"Mom," he paused for a long moment, wondering what she would say to this next question. And, secretly, being a little afraid of what she might say. "Mom, why would he do that?"

FOURTEEN

"Men. Boys. Are they all pigs?"

Wilma had just seen the dirty dishes that one of the males in her life had left on the table. She had only been gone an hour or two, and the table hadn't been like that earlier.

Upon closer examination she could tell they were from Abe. He had evidently eaten before leaving, and without asking her to fix anything for him. She wondered, yet again, what had changed with him. For the last couple of weeks he hadn't picked up a single dish and he knew how that irritated her. But his mood had been sour the whole time and she was afraid to say anything. Come to think of it, he had been drinking more lately, too. Since he was off work that day that's probably where he was right then, out drinking. Whenever his drinking had escalated before it was always a prelude to a big explosion, with her invariably ending up hurt.

After cleaning up the dishes and table she started towards the mailbox, not expecting anything special. Their mail was usually boring and of small consequence. She had no reason to suspect that day's delivery might be any different. So when she noticed some scuff marks on the floor near the front door, there was no reason to hurry to the mailbox. She prided herself on always keeping her house neat and clean and on being a good housewife and mother. Abe used to complement her about the nice home she kept for them, but that was years ago. Nary a single kind word had come from him in years.

Before long an hour had passed. She wasn't in any hurry, so a cleaning task that would have taken only a few minutes seemed to stretch out longer and longer. Then Rocky came home and she stopped to fix him a sandwich.

As soon as he sat down to eat she left the kitchen and headed for the mailbox. She felt guilty but just couldn't bring herself to be alone with him any more than was necessary. It had been two weeks since he had asked her why Clint would pay for his college and she dreaded when he might bring it up again. Back then, they had been interrupted by Abe coming home, so she had never answered her son's question. She knew that given the opportunity he would ask again and her fear kept overcoming her desire to spend time with him.

One letter immediately caught her eye. It was a plain looking envelope, hand addressed to Ms. Wilma Powlison with no return address. She saw that the postmark was from Roanoke and her heart did a flip. It wasn't her sister's handwriting on the letter, and there was only one other person she knew in Roanoke. But he wouldn't write, it just wasn't like him. Unless there was something terribly wrong. Her eyes started to tear and she went straight to her bedroom without opening the letter.

She sat in the chair in the bedroom, holding the unopened letter, tears streaming down her cheeks and her heart feeling like it was breaking.

As she sat there, the realization slowly became conscious. She had longed for Clint more and more as the years were passing by, and just recently her true feelings had begun to push into her awareness. *But just exactly what are my true feelings? Do I love him? Or is it just an attraction to someone I know I can never have? Is it all a fantasy, born from a moment of intense passion, and unconsciously nurtured all these years? Is it the connection between him and Rocky?*

Or is it all because of Abe? I don't like him anymore. I'm not even sure if I ever really loved him. He makes me, ... I can't even think it. How can a proper wife cringe when her husband is close by? It's not right. Is Clint just a transient object of my fantasy and lust? An object as unreal as any other random thoughts that go through my head? That must be it after all. I just couldn't be in love with another man. I'm a married woman and God says we're married for life, for better or worse. I'd be wise to just get over this infatuation and get back to loving my husband.

But what if I really love Clint? What if this letter says he's about to die? Or God forbid what if it's a letter from someone saying he's already dead? How could I go on living if he's dead?

No, he's just someone I think about when I'm aroused. Or when Abe is on top of me when I'm never aroused. It wouldn't matter if Clint died because I could still imagine him in place of Abe. I'm married to Abe and that's that. I'll open this stupid letter and then I'll go start making a nice dinner for my husband and son.

Just as her fingers were about to tear open the troublesome envelope she heard the commotion in the kitchen that had started a few moments before but was only just now intruding into her disturbed thoughts.

------- <<>> -------

Abe had staggered out of the bar, his face red from alcohol and anger. He was already fed up with the disrespect he had been getting from his wife and now he had just found out his son was disobeying him too.

I'll just have to teach them both some respect. She's polluted my own son and she's gonna get it. But first I'll straighten him out, all right. No son of mine is gonna embarrass me like that. And where'd he get that damn thing anyway? It must've been that old homeless jackass. Next time I see him he's gonna pay for trying to corrupt my son. They're all gonna pay. I'll teach 'em all a lesson they won't soon forget.

His anger grew with every staggering step until he tripped going up the steps to his front door and smashed his knee as he fell. The pain was instantly intense but he was a man on a mission. He wasn't going to let that stop him from dealing with the disobedience and disrespect that had become so intolerable. He slammed his way through the front door and kept going, finding Rocky in the kitchen.

"What the hell have you been doing, you little shit?" Abe's words weren't very loud, yet. But they quickly enough turned to a yell. An angry, drunken yell. "Who the hell do you think you are, anyway? Riding some damn motorcycle all over town. You knew that wasn't allowed but you did it anyway you disrespectful shit."

Wilma came around the corner just in time to see her son getting backhanded across his face. Rocky went reeling and fell backwards onto a chair and then head first to the floor. He was unconscious. Blood gushed from his nose.

Abe was a strong and tough man. He had done hard, physical work his whole life and was used to pain. So when Wilma came at him with her fists flying it didn't even slow him down. All it took from him was one blow and she fell to the floor, screaming in agony. But he wasn't done yet.

The Gold's Pharmacy manager had just heard that morning about yesterday's incident at the Powlison home and had come to the hospital as soon as he could arrange coverage at the store. Victor Zorn made a point of visiting any of his customers if they had to be in the hospital. For him it wasn't only about being the Pharmacy's manager. He genuinely cared about the welfare of all of his customers, even though his manners were quite businesslike and most people never guessed that he was really such a caring person.

The hospital nurses were well acquainted with him and were always helpful when he inquired about the medical condition of a patient. After all, as he would tell them, his pharmacy would be providing the medications for the patients after they left the hospital and he needed to know their medical histories to help avoid any drug problems. So they willingly showed him the medical charts he asked for on this visit. But the nurses were also anxious to talk, so he learned more about what had happened at the Powlison home the day before.

When he got to Wilma's room she looked surprised to see him and tried to hide her face. But it wasn't the first time he had visited an abused wife and he knew how to help put her at ease so she would feel more open to him. After some small talk they talked about Rocky, then he began gently inquiring about her intentions regarding returning to her home.

Nancy Robertson had just baked a pineapple upside down cake from a new recipe that Wilma had given her a few weeks before, and felt anxious to surprise her friend with a taste. When the taxi stopped in front of the hospital she gathered up the cake and the personal care items that Wilma had asked her to bring and headed inside. As she approached the door to Wilma's room she consciously put a smile and happy look on her face. It was a surprise to see Mr. Zorn come briskly out of Wilma's room, and he didn't stop to chat beyond just a cordial "Hello, Mrs. Robertson."

Wilma was looking at her battered and bruised face with the hand held mirror the nurse had given her when Nancy came in. Her first inclination was to hide her face from her friend, but after having become a bit more at ease with Mr. Zorn it seemed somewhat foolish to hide from her friend. So she tried to grin and bear it, even though grinning caused intense pain.

"How is he?" Nancy asked.

"The same. He's still not awake, but the doctor came by and said the test results are all good. They haven't found any permanent damage. Now it's just a matter of time until he wakes up."

"I heard they're keeping Abe in jail. So at least you won't have to worry about him hurting anyone for now."

"That's a relief. I was afraid he'd come here and try to convince me to not testify. But I'm determined to do it after what that monster did." There was no mistaking the resolve and deep anger in her voice.

Wilma continued with small talk. After she had calmed down some they enjoyed some of Nancy's pineapple upside down cake. Wilma was quick to tell her friend how delicious it was. After a while Nancy mentioned that she had seen Mr. Zorn, hoping that Wilma would volunteer as to why he had been there.

"He told me I can stay in the apartment above the Pharmacy if I don't want to go back to the house. He's much kinder than I had thought."

"Is that what you're going to do?"

"I think so. I don't think I could stand to go home right now. Not with the, the, ... mess everywhere." She paused, then continued, "He said it's modest but comfortable and that no one's there during the warm weather. They only use it when it snows bad and someone has to stay over to open the store in the morning."

"I wonder why he would offer it to you. He seems so stiff and standoffish. Did he say anything about that?"

"No, he didn't," she lied, not wanting to tell anyone what Mr. Zorn had actually said. "But he did say there's an extra room that can be used as a bedroom with room enough for Rocky and that he would arrange for another bed to be delivered." Wilma held back the tears, then continued, "I just hope Rocky can be there real soon." Now the tears couldn't be held back any longer.

After the crying stopped, Nancy gave her the personal care things she had brought for her. Then Wilma decided to share with her friend what her injuries were. She told her about the broken arm, bruised ribs, badly bruised but thankfully not broken nose and face, and her cracked teeth.

Just as she finished describing her condition, the doctor came in and surprised her with the news that she could go home. The x-rays hadn't shown any more damage so she would be just fine as soon as everything healed. But she would need to follow up with her doctor and, of course, her dentist.

"Well then, let's get moving," Nancy said. "I'll help you and we'll have you over to the Pharmacy in no time."

On their way out of the hospital the ladies stopped for a time to sit with Rocky. Wilma liked to talk to him and hoped he could hear her. Maybe that would help him wake up sooner. She planned to tell him the things that had been kept secret, but that would have to wait until the two of them were alone.

Mr. Zorn rushed back to the Pharmacy as there were many things to be done to prepare for the new residents. He would have helped Wilma and Rocky even without any instructions from his boss, but he wouldn't have offered them the apartment upstairs. But, as he had explained to Wilma, Clint had left written instructions with him specifying that he should give them any assistance they needed or asked for. Based on how firm the instructions had been, he felt that Clint's intention would include the apartment and whatever else they might need. He couldn't help wondering if Clint had some premonition that something bad might happen in the Powlison household and wanted to make sure Wilma and Rocky would be provided for.

He was truly a man of his word. Immediately upon returning to work he sent two employees up to the apartment to make sure it was clean and the bed made. As soon as they were done he gave them the key to Wilma's car, which she had given to him, and sent them to bring her car to the Pharmacy. Meanwhile he arranged to have a telephone installed upstairs, made sure the refrigerator was well stocked, and selected the first aid products he thought she might need from the store's shelves and took them upstairs. He kept a careful record of everything he took from the store up to the apartment, not because he would ever expect Wilma to pay but because he was a stickler about keeping a good inventory record.

He wanted to call his boss and apprise him of what had happened but Wilma had begged him not to, and he didn't think it would help Clint to hear such things right now. So he would refrain, at least for a while.

Once those things were taken care of he could get away to go purchase a bed for the den. He just hoped and prayed that it would be used, and the sooner the better.

FIFTEEN

Wilma had a painful evening and night, barely sleeping. Her body hurt something awful. She hurt everywhere Abe had hit her, not just where there was obvious damage. Her thoughts kept going to her husband, wondering how he could have been so awful. She had trouble believing it had been him doing those things to her and Rocky. He had hit her before, but never more than once or twice at a time. And never so hard, except for that one time that she didn't like to remember. She hadn't had so many broken bones before, or a smashed face.

But worst of all was what he had done to Rocky. Before she passed out from the onslaught and crippling pain she heard Abe cursing about the motorcycle and about Clint. So somehow he had found out about Rocky's purchase. But how? Someone must have seen Rocky on Teaser and told him about it.

During one of her many wakeful moments before the sun came up, she vowed, *that son-of-a-bitch isn't going to take Teaser away from my boy. In fact, just as soon as Rocky wakes up I'm going to get him to take me for a ride on Teaser. And Abe can just go to hell.*

As soon as she awoke for good that morning she set about getting ready to go visit her son. Then later she would decide if she felt up to going to her house to get some of her things. She hadn't been in the kitchen since the paramedics had taken her and Rocky in the ambulances, and she didn't know if she could face up to seeing the blood just yet.

Checking around the apartment she noticed for the first time that Mr. Zorn had stocked the kitchen and refrigerator for her, and on the bedroom dresser he had arranged first aid supplies for her injuries. The bathroom even had toiletries and personal care items, and two fresh new toothbrushes. He truly was an angel for her right now. Without his help she didn't know what she would have done. He had told her it was a modest apartment, but right now it had become a safe haven and she thought it looked very grand indeed.

Her pain medications made her a bit too woozy to drive so she decided to take a taxi to the hospital to sit with Rocky. But since the phone wouldn't be installed until that afternoon she went downstairs to use the pay phone on the front porch of the pharmacy, then went around back and waited where she would be out of sight.

Once at Rocky's side she began telling him all about Clint. She even told him the answer to the question he had asked not too long ago but that she had never answered, which was just why Clint would be interested in paying for his college expenses. That was really hard for her to talk about, but she forced herself to say all of it. Since he couldn't ask any questions and wasn't able to judge or criticize her, she felt free to elaborate at length about all of it.

Throughout the morning, while talking to Rocky, she felt that he was stirring just a bit and could somehow hear her. She hoped so, even though what she was telling him at length would be quite a shock to him. It was time that he knew everything. Especially now, after what Abe had done to him.

Later, as Wilma prepared to go eat lunch in the hospital cafeteria, she straightened up the chair she had been sitting in and glanced back over at her son just before leaving the room and gasped. He was in a different position! His head had turned slightly and his arm had moved! She hadn't actually seen him move, but she was sure of it anyway. "Rocky, Rocky," she said, "please wake up, my darling."

Rocky had been drifting in and out of consciousness since daybreak. The deep confusion he felt was scary and disturbing. But slowly he began to remember some of what had happened in his kitchen. He remembered his father yelling and cursing and coming at him. Then he remembered his father hitting him, hard. After that he couldn't remember any details.

He thought that he must be dead. But no, if he were dead then he could open his eyes and see God.

Gradually he sensed the confusion clearing somewhat and he could hear some talking around him. Sounded like nurses, maybe. Touching him. He felt them touching his arm. He realized he must be alive. And probably in a hospital.

He needed to open his eyes. He could barely get them opened before going asleep again. He tried many times, but only made slight progress. Gradually he managed to stay awake more, but still couldn't get his eyes to open any wider than just a slit. Even so, that slit of opening helped him confirm that he was indeed in a hospital.

Then he started wondering if he could move any of his body but gave that up after every attempt just sent him back asleep. All of this wore him out, so he thought he'd just lie there for awhile, staying awake as much as possible but without moving. He tried to focus on the frequent voices he could hear coming from the hallway and guessed that the room he was in must be by the nurse's station.

He sensed someone in the room but didn't try to open his eyes because he thought that would just put him asleep again, so he focused on listening to try to figure out what was going on. Then he heard his mother's voice. She was talking to him just as if he were awake. He knew it was her and he could understand her individual words. But he still had some trouble staying focused and alert so her sentences didn't always make sense to him.

She told him that it wasn't his father that had hit him. When she told him that Clint was his real father it didn't register right away. Then as it began to sink in he realized that she had stopped talking. He made a monumental effort to wake up and even tried to sit up, but then he fell into sleep again, barely hearing her saying to please wake up.

It had been extremely difficult for Wilma to discuss what had happened with the policemen and the others that had interviewed her. They had come to the hospital earlier that day and spent a long time with her. She had recounted everything she remembered in as much detail as she could muster. They also spoke with the doctor and hospital staff about her and Rocky. One of the men told her that she would need to testify against her husband and asked how she felt about that. She forcefully told him that anyone who would hurt her son and herself that way deserved to stay in jail no matter how hard it would be for her to testify.

She had returned to the apartment about mid-afternoon. Then around dinnertime she heard someone knocking on the door. Not expecting anyone, she felt a sudden and powerful fear envelop and paralyze her. What if it was Abe? What if he was already out of jail and had come to beat her again?

"Wilma? Wilma, are you here?"

Wilma's relief was so instantaneous and profound that she crumpled right down to the floor. By the time she got to her feet again she had to rush to the door and just caught Nancy before she got back into the taxi. "Nancy, come on up," she yelled down.

"Oh good. You're here. I brought some dinner for us. I'll be up soon as I pay the driver."

During the delicious dinner that her friend had prepared, she told Nancy all about her day with Rocky.

How he had moved that morning, and during the afternoon his eyes had opened several times. And how excited she had been when one time he moved his eyes and found hers. She said, "He's going to be alright. I just know it. He's going to be fine."

A while later Nancy told her, "I went over to your house today. I hope you don't mind. I just couldn't stand to think of you having to clean up after what happened to you and Rocky."

Just then Mr. Zorn knocked on the door, inquiring as to how Wilma was doing and how young Rocky was. He informed Wilma that Rocky's bed would be delivered the next day. Then he said he was going home for the evening and mentioned that he had seen Ms. Robertson arrive in a taxi and offered her a ride home if she were ready to leave.

After they left Wilma thought about how blessed she was to have a good friend like Nancy and an unexpected angel in Mr. Zorn. Together they were making this whole experience much easier to bear. If only Clint could be there too, she thought. It was the first time ever that she had thought about wanting Clint to be with her when she didn't also think about how impossible such a thing would be.

Wilma put on the TV and took a pain pill. She was determined not to take any more of them during the night so she could drive herself to the hospital in the morning. But if it were anything like the night before, she would be taking another pain pill every 4 hours all night long. Either way, it was going to be a long night.

------- <<>> -------

As night fell Rocky drifted asleep again. Without the room lights on and without the sunshine coming in the window he quickly lost the battle with sleep. But at first daylight he was awake again. The nurses hadn't bothered to draw the shade and the east-facing window brightened the whole room.

He awoke with his face towards the sun and his eyes squinting against the brightness. He turned his head away from the window and opened his eyes without even realizing how momentous an occurrence that was. The only thing he thought about was the most parched throat he had ever felt and where could he get some water. It wasn't until he reached for the nurse call button that he realized how lousy yesterday had been and how he felt so much better today.

They would only give him a sip of water but a pretty young nurse smiled at him and said she'd stay and give him another sip in a few minutes. Seeing such a pretty smile directed only at him convinced him that he was really alive after all. He adjusted his covers so she wouldn't continue to see just how really alive he actually was.

A couple of hours later, but still early in the morning, he finally convinced the pretty nurse that he could walk to the bathroom, which she allowed him to do with her assistance. He was just coming out of the bathroom when his mother arrived and ran to hug him. They hadn't called her right away with the great news about Rocky being wide-awake because they needed to talk with the doctor first. As soon as they could reach him he told them to go ahead and call her and she had rushed straight over.

Later that morning his doctor said he might be able to go home the next day and that there was no sign of permanent damage. The doctor also said he could likely return to school in time to finish up the school year with his classmates. But for now he needed to rest and to only gradually add activities leading back towards his regular routine.

------- <<>> -------

Mr. Zorn was delighted to hear the news about Rocky, and he told Wilma so. She then explained how her son had spent the day getting more and more stir crazy in the hospital room and could hardly wait to be released the next morning. They were in the Pharmacy and Wilma had stopped by on her way from the hospital to the apartment upstairs. He told her that Rocky's bed had been delivered earlier that day and that it was now all prepared with linens and a blanket.

"Do you think it would be ok if I stop over to see him this evening after work?" he asked.

"Oh, Mr. Zorn, I know he'd love to have another visitor. After I was there all day with him I think he was getting a bit tired of me."

"Good. Then I'll just go ahead on over to see him right now. That way I'll be back in time to lock up the store later."

"Before you go, I have a favor to ask. I don't know anyone that can do it for me, but I'm hoping you might have some ideas." After she told him what she wanted, he said he didn't know anyone that could do it either, but would see what he could do.

"Mom, how did Teaser get here?" he excitedly asked.

"I asked Mr. Zorn if he could do me a big favor and arrange it somehow, and this morning Gus Marshall from Gus's Gas brought her over on his truck. Gus said he found her behind the garage just where I thought she might be. I wanted her to be here for you."

Wilma and Rocky had just pulled up behind Gold's Pharmacy. Rocky was well enough that the doctor had let him check out that morning but insisted that he go straight home and rest as much as possible during the day. Wilma had managed to reduce her pain pills during the night even though she was still in a lot of pain, especially towards the end of each day. She wanted to be able to drive him home if the doctor would allow it. Now here they were, and she had wanted Teaser to be part of his homecoming.

"I guess you know all about Teaser," he said.

"Yes, dear, your Uncle Clint told me about selling her to you."

"He's not my uncle."

"No, dear."

"Mom, after we get upstairs will you tell me all about Clint?" He hesitated, then added, "and about you, too?"

SIXTEEN

The room was modestly but comfortably furnished, with a small table and two chairs, a desk and chair, TV, adequate lighting, and a single bed. The walls were painted and papered in bright, cheerful colors and designs, as were the walls in the private bathroom. It wasn't anything like a typical hospital room. Both windows had nice blinds and a view of the pleasantly landscaped grounds. There were several dozen such rooms, each similar to the others.

The nurse's station, situated just off the main entry lobby, was modern and unobtrusive. There were usually four or five nurses on duty during the day and two at night. A few of the patients required a lot of nursing care but most were self-sufficient and needed only limited assistance and care.

There were several shared areas, including a dining room, TV and game room with card tables and a billiards table, and a lounge. A separate, smaller wing held examination rooms, chemotherapy rooms, doctor's offices, administrative offices, and a kitchen.

Clint's room, like the others, was his full time home while in residence. The private hospital served both in and outpatients, but the private rooms were for the inpatients like Clint. His doctor had advised him to stay inpatient for two months and then they would evaluate his progress and the side effects of his drug regimen. With very limited access to cancer treatment in Johnson's Crossing he wouldn't be able to go back there until his treatments were much further along. The medical insurance that Clint and Mr. Zorn provided for employees and management at the Pharmacy paid a good portion of the inpatient costs and Clint's personal wealth made up the difference without any problem.

He had chosen a room with a view of Mill Mountain and the Roanoke Star. He and Meredith had been up there many times for picnics and necking so it had happy memories for him. And right now he wanted as many happy memories as he could find. With his new attitude about his past, memories that once had been so painful were now happy. Clint chuckled at the thought of how just a short time ago he would have felt profound sadness thinking about kissing Meredith under the Star, but now it was a happy memory. Very, very good progress, he thought.

At first he had been really tired and nauseated from the treatments so he stayed in his room almost all of the time. But as the doctor adjusted his meds he felt better and was able to spend time every day in the shared areas and had begun to enjoy the company of the other patients. Everyone had their own story and it was usually inspiring for him to hear them. As the weeks passed he had spent less and less time locked in his past when Meredith was still alive. The present offered him activities and companionship as well as both hope and excitement for his future. He was becoming a new person.

After a couple of weeks he had begun going outside every day, briefly at first. The grounds were nicely designed and maintained. Many of the patients enjoyed getting outside for short periods each day and there were places to sit in the sun or shade, as desired. He also began to look forward to taking some short excursions off campus and hoped that could happen soon but he knew he wasn't quite ready just yet.

------- <<>> -------

"I remember you saying that Clint is my real father. Did you say that or was I dreaming?" Rocky had decided to skip the preliminaries and ask his mom the most important question and get that part over with.

They were sitting at the kitchen table in the Pharmacy's apartment. Wilma had shown him the apartment and how she and Mr. Zorn had prepared a room for him, but he had hardly noticed. His mind was on something more important and he had quickly brought her to the table and sat down.

"Yes, he's your real father," she said. "I should've told you before but I couldn't figure out how to do it. Then while you were in a coma I knew I couldn't wait any longer no matter what."

"So you told me while you thought I was unconscious and wouldn't hear you?"

"Oh honey, I'm so sorry. I love you so much. I didn't want to hurt you but I didn't know how else to do it. Please forgive me for not telling you sooner. But I just couldn't bring myself to do it."

"So what if I had been unconscious and hadn't heard you? Would you have told me when I woke up or would you have chickened out again?" he said angrily. He knew there were other questions that he needed to ask but he felt very angry that she had told him while he laid there helpless.

"I'm sorry. I wish I had had the courage to do it differently." She was feeling detached from the discussion and was surprised at how calm she felt.

"Does Dad know?" He felt awkward saying Dad but Abe had been his dad for his entire life until that moment and he didn't know how else to say it.

"I think he used to suspect. Maybe he still suspects. I don't know. But I don't think he ever knew for sure. I guess I never had the courage to talk to him about it either."

He bolted from the table without a word and went to his room, slamming the door behind him.

She sat there not knowing what to do. She hadn't been prepared for how to deal with the situation, and then his just leaving like that left her stunned. She had thought they would discuss it until he had all his questions answered, but now she was realizing that it wasn't going to be over with so quickly. Unable to stay detached and calm any longer, the sobs rose quickly from her heart and she collapsed onto her arms on the table. Somewhere in the recesses of her mind she realized that her previous demeanor had been a fearful façade. But much more troubling was the feeling that she had probably lost her son forever and had only herself to blame for it.

The day was passing ever so slowly. Finally it was lunchtime and Wilma set about preparing a meal for Rocky and herself. He hadn't come out of his room and she thought she had heard him crying earlier, but otherwise it was deathly quiet and lonely in the apartment. She planned to make the meal and then hope that he would allow her to talk with him some more. But she couldn't help feeling that any plans she made would probably go awry and she'd never get him back.

"Rocky, dear," she said while knocking gently on his door, "I made lunch for us. Would you come out and we can eat?" She sat at the kitchen table, not knowing quite what to do. Then, to her great relief, Rocky came to the table and sat down.

"Why?" was the only thing he said.

She quickly tried to figure out what he meant. Why did she fix lunch? Why did she want him to come out? What was it that he wanted to know? Then, like a ton of bricks, she realized that he was asking why she had slept with Clint. Like everything else about this whole problem, she hadn't planned how to answer a question like that.

"I'm not sure how to answer that," was all she could muster.

"You could try just telling me the truth for a change," he said.

She suddenly knew what she had to do. Her son was old enough to understand feelings so she needed to be completely truthful now. "When Abe and I first married his drinking wasn't a problem. He drank some on his days off, but it didn't seem like too much. Maybe

I was just naive but it seemed ok. I knew some other wives that had husbands that drank more, and that ran around with other women. So Abe didn't seem so bad."

Now that she had started, it was easier to keep going. After a moment's pause she continued, "I was working at the Pharmacy back then. Clint was my boss. That was before he started going downhill. I got promoted to assistant manager and after that there were lots of times I had to stay late if they were short handed. But I loved my job and Clint was easy to work with and we became good friends." She paused, as if remembering the good times, then continued, "Abe didn't like me staying late because he wanted his dinner ready at a certain time. He started yelling at me about coming home late even though the extra money helped us out. It got to where I knew if I stayed late he'd be mad and drunk by the time I got home. Then he started to hit me." The tears couldn't be held back any longer. She got up and got a clean dishtowel to dry her face with then sat back down and continued.

"At first he would always apologize and then he'd be extra nice to me for awhile. But then he wasn't so nice, and then the apologies stopped too. That's also when his hitting me started to really hurt. Before they weren't so awful, just some bruises. But they got worse and worse. Then one night he hit me so hard he broke three ribs." Wilma was sobbing by that time.

Rocky just sat there, not knowing what to say or do. He had himself been hit plenty of times by Abe, but never in a way that might have broken a bone. At least not until the other day when Abe had knocked him unconscious. Yet, somehow, he had always known that if he pushed his dad too hard the consequences would have been a lot more severe. Hearing that Abe had broken his mother's ribs made him angry, even angrier than he had been at her for what she had done. So, he realized, when his father had just broken some of her bones it wasn't the first time he had been horribly violent with her. He hesitantly reached his hand over to his mom's shoulder while she continued to sob.

Every time Abe had hit her, he had wanted to kill his father. Sitting there at the table he realized just how deep that anger was. It wasn't a conscious realization, but he knew that the anger was more pervasive than he had ever admitted to himself before. Somehow he was angrier at his father for hitting his mom than for having knocked him unconscious. His mom had always been kind and loving to him, and to Abe too, for that matter, and the idea that his father had broken her ribs so many years ago was almost more than he could bear. But bear it he must, for right now he needed to hear more about what had happened.

She started talking again. "He was so drunk he couldn't drive me to the hospital so I drove myself. It hurt so bad I don't know how I managed to do it but I did. After they treated me and wrapped my chest I didn't know what to do. I couldn't go home. I was just too scared. He might've hit me again. Besides, I really hated him right then and didn't want to be in the same house with him." She stopped talking for a few moments and caught her breath.

"I couldn't go to any of my friends either. I couldn't let them know what had happened. Not that my own husband had hit me so hard it broke my ribs. So I went to the only place where I felt safe."

"To Clint?" he asked.

"He had a house just down the block from here. I went there and he gave me his room and he slept on the couch. He had always been nice to me. I'm sure he had some feelings for me but he wouldn't have ever said anything because I was married. Clint's always been kind and honest. Not like Abe." She had to stop for a minute, so she went for a glass of water as an excuse for a brief break. But soon she continued again.

"The next day I barely got out of bed, then the day after that I went to work even though I could barely walk around. Clint told me to take more time off but I couldn't stand to just sit around and feel sorry for myself. But I was still afraid to go home so Clint insisted I stay at his house again. After he fixed us dinner we were watching TV and I sat close beside him on the couch. I wasn't planning anything. At least I don't think I was. But he had been so loving to me that I just started to kiss him. I just wanted to feel loved and not afraid anymore."

"At first he told me to stop. But I could tell then that he had real feelings for me. I just really wanted to feel close to him so I kept on. After awhile we went to bed together. The next day I was off work and I went home. I wouldn't tell Abe where I had been for three nights, but I did tell him he'd better never hit me again. We made up and it was like a honeymoon again. At least for a little while, anyway. Then you were born. Abe didn't hit me for a long time, but then when you were little he started again."

"But how do you know Clint's my father? Couldn't you have gotten pregnant from Dad?"

"Oh, honey, it's just so many things. Your blue eyes, your blond hair, your nose, even your disposition.

But I knew right away even before you were born. That's why I named you Tom - it's your real father's middle name. Then when you were a toddler you had to have some blood tests because of an infection and I saw your blood type. There's no doubt about it. But I want you to know that I've always loved you. You're my son no matter what. Do you hear me? You're *my* son. And I love you." She went over to where he was sitting and hugged him, tears streaming all over his shoulder.

"I know, Mom. And I love you too. But I'm pretty confused right now." He was crying too.

Wilma kept tossing and turning, completely unable to sleep. After the things she had told her son she felt relieved but knew it would take some time for him to sort it out. He had gone to his room after their talk and they hadn't had any significant conversation for the rest of the day or evening. She had fixed him some dinner but he took it to his room to eat in privacy. She tried to convince herself that it was all going to be all right because he hadn't been nasty to her during the rest of the day, and hadn't seemed angry, but she still worried that she had lost him forever.

She also kept worrying about what to do about Abe. She hated him right then, but he was still her husband. And still Rocky's dad, too, for that matter. And still the breadwinner, if they gave him his job back after being in jail, that is. After hours of worry she decided that she couldn't make any decisions about Abe until later. She knew if she made a decision right then it would be to go and kill him for what he had done. Better to sleep on it, she told herself. As if she could sleep, anyway.

She also worried about how to get some money coming in. Even though Mr. Zorn had made it very clear that the apartment was free, she would still have expenses. *And for Rocky too, if he stays with me after all that's happened. What a horrible thought, **if** he stays with me. Of course he'll stay. He has to. I couldn't bear it if he ran away from me. He just has to stay.*

Somewhere during the night she decided that she wasn't going to live in her house again, ever. *Just the thought of being there makes me afraid. That means I need to look for a job. I'll talk with Mr. Zorn in the morning, perhaps he knows of someone in town that's hiring.*

And in a couple of days maybe Rocky will be ready to go back to school. Everything will be all right then. He and I will be back to normal. It will all be all right then. With that thought she drifted off to a restless sleep.

Rocky wasn't sleeping either. He tried sitting in the chair in his room, then lying on the bed, sitting on the floor, but nothing worked. He couldn't get comfortable and he couldn't stop his mind from running overtime.

Learning that Clint was his real father hadn't been as much of a shock as he would have thought. He had never felt real close to Abe and they didn't look alike. Clint had always treated him special. *Maybe I had a subconscious thought that Clint's my father. Maybe that's why it wasn't so shocking. Or maybe I wanted Clint to be my father instead of Dad.*

Even so, he couldn't relax and sleep. *What do I do now? Stop calling Abe dad? That might not matter anyway since I don't want to ever see him again. But it feels funny to call Clint dad. So what now?*

He wanted to see Clint and talk to him. He didn't know what he was going to say, but he wanted to talk with him anyway.

And what about Mom? She cheated on Dad. But if she hadn't done that I wouldn't even be here. It's so confusing.

After hours of mind chatter he did decide that his mom wasn't so awful for what she had done. His dad had hit him and now he didn't want to ever see him again, so how must Mom have felt when he hit her and broke her ribs? *It's no wonder she didn't feel safe with him and did feel safe with Clint. I don't feel safe about Dad right now either.*

He decided to take Teaser for a ride the next day. He would ride up into the mountains and just learn how to ride her better. *Just her and me, on the road together.* He finally drifted off to sleep.

SEVENTEEN

"The doctor said I can leave the grounds today," he said from the chair in the corner of the room.

Clint's favorite nurse ignored him while she straightened the sheets and covers on his bed. Finally he said it again only louder this time, "The doctor said I can leave the grounds today!"

"Heard you the first time," she said. "I'm not as old as you are. I can hear just fine."

"So why the hell didn't you answer me?"

"Because you didn't ask me a question. If you had asked me a question, then I might have answered you. Or not. But you made a statement. You didn't ask me a question." She finished with the bed and started setting up to draw a blood sample from Clint's arm.

He knew from his history with her over the last month that she was always ready to joke with him or to challenge him. He wasn't sure at that moment which it was this time. So he thought he'd just wait a few moments to see if she was going to continue.

"I don't think he told you that. I think you're staying here all day just like yesterday and the day before. But you might be happy to know that I get to leave early today and my husband is taking me to a nice restaurant. You can think about that while you're still here." She stuck the needle in his vein.

He knew it was all intended to get him sparing with her, but he wasn't going to take the bait. Besides, he had seen her reading the doctor's orders for the day so she already knew he was telling the truth. He said, "But I won't be here. I told you the doctor said I can go out today."

"Are you sure he said that? I think you're just making stuff up like you always do. I think you're just trying to get me to help you break outta here. Well it ain't going to happen."

"He said it, all right. And I'm doing it. Just as fast as I can get you to finish up with that damn needle," he chided.

"Watch it buster, or I'll miss your vein on purpose. Then we'll see what happens to smart alecks like you," she teased back.

"You miss a vein and you won't be my favorite anymore."

"Funny boy. I haven't been anybody's favorite since I used to sponge bathe old Mr. Unger," she laughingly said.

"You can just skip this blood test anyway. You don't really need any more of my blood. I've already given plenty of samples. My arms are sore from the needles."

"There you go, mister impatience. All done. So where are you going, anyway?" she asked while marking the blood vial with the name Clint Larkins.

"I think I'll take a taxi to whatever popular shopping street the driver recommends and then just sit on a bench and people watch."

"Sounds exciting," she said mockingly.

"It beats sitting here and getting stabbed by you all day. But if you're nice I might bring you a present."

"Bring the present first, then I'll see if it's worth being nice."

The nurse left and Clint called for a taxi, then went to the main entryway of the private hospital to wait. This would be his first time off the grounds and he was looking forward to being in public on his inaugural trip after many years of looking like an unkempt bum, or worse. He had gotten back into the habit of daily hygiene over the last month and it now felt good to be clean and look nice. He didn't plan to do any shopping on this outing, but figured he'd look for a couple of stores that he could go to on another day and expand his wardrobe beyond the meager selection the hospital had gotten for him.

Clint's graying, formerly blond hair had all fallen out but he thought that he looked rather handsome with a smooth head. Once he got used to the shock of his drug induced baldness he decided there was no need to hide his head under a cap. Since coming to the hospital he had been watching a few movies on TV and had seen several men around his age that were completely bald, and they usually seemed to be attractive to the actresses in the movies, so why not him? He was, after all, a tall and reasonably handsome man for his age, with blue eyes that had begun to regain some of their former intensity of color.

His biggest concern was that he would become overly fatigued while away from his temporary home. But he felt fairly confident that should the need arise he would be able to get a taxi to take him back without too much of a delay. The fatigue was with him every day, sometimes quite severely, but on other days it was only a nuisance. The most severe side effect from the drugs was nausea but the doctor kept gradually reducing the dosage of the one that caused most of that so he was getting some relief there. All in all he was very pleased with how everything was progressing and how he had begun changing his life back to that of a normal person and not a sad old bum that lived in the long ago past.

This was also a preparatory jaunt. He felt that getting away for a few hours would brighten his mood and broaden the topics of conversation that he would be able to have soon with Wilma and Rocky. He was looking forward to their visit in 3 days, which had been scheduled with his treatment plan in mind so he wouldn't be too fatigued when they came.

Over the last month he had spoken with Wilma many times on the phone, and several times with Rocky. He had never been much for phone conversation but had been making a heroic effort to be sociable on the phone with the two people in this world that he loved. Still, he couldn't help being nervous about the visit, since Wilma had told him about her conversations with Rocky.

------- <<>> -------

It's good to be back at work again, Abe Powlison thought to himself. *Never could stand being kept in one place. That must be what hell's like.*

He had spent two weeks in jail, then another couple of weeks meeting with his court appointed lawyer and psychologist to get a clearance before Johnson's Refinery would let him return to work. They wanted to be certain that he wasn't a danger to others. He had, after all, beat up his wife and put his son in a coma. His boss told him he was lucky they were critically short handed of experienced people or he wouldn't have taken him back at all.

The psychologist made him start going to an out-patient alcohol treatment facility and to an anger management support group. Between the lawyer, psychologist, and alcohol counselor, they had all made it very clear that if he were to have any hope at all of getting a suspended sentence then he'd better stay sober and stay in those programs. He had assured them that he would do whatever it took to get his life back together and to reunite with his family.

He had tried several times after getting out of jail to see Wilma and Rocky but at first he didn't know where they were. It took him a few days to find them staying above Gold's Pharmacy, but then they both refused to see him. His lawyer had told him that since there had been no restraining order filed he could legally go to see them, but that he'd better be very careful and not do anything to make them feel threatened in any way. And he sure didn't want to do anything that would get him put back in that hell of a jail.

Wilma had called him once at the house to ask when he would be gone so she could come by to get some things, and they had talked for a few minutes. He had told her how very sorry he was and that he hoped and prayed that she and Rocky could forgive him so they could go back to being a family again. He had asked to speak with Rocky but she said it wasn't time yet for that. At least he found out that both of them would heal from their injuries. If Rocky hadn't come out of his coma ok it would have been more than he could bear.

Abe wasn't a man to show emotions and he tried not to feel them either, except when he had been drinking, and this situation was taxing him beyond anything he had ever experienced. He wanted his family back but the pain of what he had done was almost too much to bear. His doctor had given him some pills that helped, but it was still awful for him.

Wilma had often told him, back in the old days when they talked more, that she loved how reliable he was and she always knew she could depend on him to earn a living for their family. When Rocky came along they decided that she would be a stay-at-home mom so she reluctantly quit the assistant manager job that she loved at Gold's Pharmacy. He didn't have an education so his job at the Refinery was the best he would ever be able to do, and it paid enough to provide for them and had good benefits.

He had grown up being taught that family was the most important thing in a man's life and he took his family and responsibilities seriously. If it weren't for his drinking problem he wouldn't be in the pickle he was in. But now he was determined to kick the bottle and make AA a part of his life, and to win back his family.

Whatever it took, that's what he would do. Anything to get his family back together again. He kept thinking "I love them" over and over.

The busy area in the heart of downtown Roanoke hustled and bustled with the comings and goings of countless people. Clint made a game of picking out individuals and trying to guess if each was perhaps a local worker, a shopper, or maybe a tourist passing through the heart of Virginia on his or her way to some other destination. Even though the high level of activity on the street and sidewalk was alien to everything he had known for the last dozens of years, he felt enthralled with the vibrancy of it all.

He discovered that Roanoke hadn't developed much of a downtown shopping district, unlike some towns and cities where the civic leaders worked to encourage such things. But the taxi driver had recommended Market Street as a place where he could sit in front of a coffee shop and people watch. The old time produce mart attracted a variety of people. From his table and chair on the sidewalk in front of the coffee shop he immensely enjoyed the world passing by in front of him. He didn't have the energy to join them as they scurried along like ants that had found a new food source, but watching them was great sport. It took his mind off his sickness for a time, and anything that did that was good for him.

With spring in full bloom the motorcycle riders had come out of their wintry confinements and seemed to be enjoying their annual ritual of new freedom, even amidst the throngs of traffic and tall buildings. Vehicle traffic wasn't allowed through the two blocks of produce stands, but his table was at the end of the mart and adjacent to a busy road. Every time he heard a motorcycle he turned to look at it and its driver. This behavior amused him because he certainly wouldn't know any of those bikers, yet he had to turn to look at every single one of them. He was quite pleased that he had sold Teaser to Rocky, but with every rumble of a big V-twin's exhaust he felt a pang of desire.

He saw a candy stand amidst the busy market and had enough energy to go and select a nice assortment for the staff at the hospital, and another assortment for his favorite nurse.

A bit later, during the taxi ride back, he began to think about Wilma and Rocky and what they had been through. She had told him all about it on the phone and warned him that her face didn't look its best yet but she wanted to visit him anyway. Rocky had also told him he wanted to visit, and to talk to him about something important. This of course thrilled Clint and he was looking forward to their visit more than he had looked forward to anything in decades. He didn't care how Wilma looked. She was always pretty to him.

For the rest of that day, and the next, his thoughts kept returning to Wilma and Rocky. He fantasized about what it might be like if they were all one family. He and Meredith had wanted children, and now here was Rocky who might, just maybe, accept him as his father. And Wilma, gentle kind Wilma, would she consider him as a husband, maybe?

Wilma had always reminded him of Meredith in so many ways, but he hadn't consciously realized it until just recently. Both women had gone out of their way to be kind and thoughtful to him, in a way that was unlike any of the other women he had known. On the surface they didn't look anything like each other. But their blue/green eyes were almost identical and the shape of their noses and mouths were actually quite similar. They had similar slender builds with breasts that were high and pert. But what intrigued him more than any of that was how similar their personalities were in some ways. Both had a sly sense of humor and loved to laugh, were quick with a slightly sarcastic but harmless comment when the opportunity arose, and were very bright and quick witted. And they both had seen the inner person within him and they liked what they saw.

As the days in rehab passed he became more consciously aware of just how much the two women were alike. And just how much he felt towards Wilma. It made sense to him that he would want her, just as he had wanted Meredith so many years before. If he did this right he could have her, too, he told himself. And hopefully Rocky would accept him, also. Then reality would set in and he'd just say "silly thoughts" to himself.

Still, he kept coming back to thinking "I love them" over and over.

EIGHTEEN

That's startling, she thought. Our features are so much alike. Our eyes are the same blue/green. And look at our noses and mouths. My hair's dark but both of us have straight hair. It's amazing.

Wilma had just been looking at some pictures of Meredith in Clint's old photo album and had been so startled that she had taken one of the closeups to the mirror and compared it to her own face. She and Meredith shared many features. She already knew they had similar body shapes, although hers would never compare to the perfect curves of Meredith's. Still, they were similar in many ways.

That's so interesting. Meredith was an absolutely beautiful woman and we look alike in many ways. But I'm anything but beautiful. Interesting.

And we both love Clint.

I know I love him, but do I love him as someone that has always been kind towards me, or as I would love a lover or husband? Not like Abe, but a husband that I could truly love? When I fantasize about Clint I feel wonderful all over and my body reacts intensely. But is that lust or love?

It must be love. I've fantasized lustfully about other men but it's never made my whole body feel like when I think about being intimate with Clint.

I've always been fond of him. Ever since I first worked for him so many years ago. And I don't think I would have slept with him that night if I hadn't secretly loved him even then. Maybe we're supposed to be together now and maybe that's why he's taking care of himself again. I think I'd like being together with him. It feels good to think about. Very interesting.

Enough of that now. I have to get ready for work.

Wilma didn't like working a split shift. But it was the only thing available at the Pharmacy when she had spoken with Mr. Zorn about a job. Together they had worked out a schedule so she would be home upstairs in the apartment for Rocky after school, then home again late in the evening. And even when she wasn't home, she would be just downstairs if he needed her for anything. She still felt very protective of her son even though several months had passed since Abe had attacked both of them.

Abe was back at the Refinery, working his old job with its frequent shift changes. She had met him one day a couple of weeks ago for lunch. He told her he wanted her and Rocky back and that he would do anything to prove himself to her. He begged her to come home. He swore he would never drink again. He begged, and he promised.

She told him no, but then relented under his pressure and promises, and agreed to think about it. But she had been strong and forceful in telling him that she would stay living where she was while she thought about it, and would complete moving her things from the house. She made numerous trips to the house, always when Abe was at work, and moved all of her and Rocky's things to the storage area behind the apartment that Mr. Zorn had so kindly cleared out for them.

Rocky had returned to his regular school schedule and his teachers had all helped him catch up on his missed work. He rode Teaser to school every day, even when it rained, and it seemed to Wilma that he loved that old motorcycle more than anything or anyone. She had insisted that he attend a motorcycle riding class at a dealership in Roanoke. They had both gone to the class, her driving her car into the city with Rocky instructed to ride behind her car and not do anything crazy. The class went very well and he seemed to have a natural talent that made it easy for him. Wilma, for her part, did all of the classroom work along with the other students, and even rode a small motorcycle that the dealership provided. She didn't pass the class, but she got what she wanted from the experience and felt much better about Rocky's riding. Even though she would never be a rider herself, now she knew some of what it felt like for him and could share in his experiences when he talked with her about his day almost every evening.

They had become much closer since the estrangement from Abe. Rocky seemed very protective of her, even as she was protective of him. He had visited Clint in Roanoke almost every weekend and had even referred to him as Dad once to her. They rarely spoke about Abe.

Wilma visited Clint on every single one of her days off work. She usually worked weekends, so she would see him during the week. With Rocky going to Roanoke on the weekends and her seeing Clint twice during the week, he was getting four visits most weeks. Then two things happened that would change Wilma's and Rocky's lives forever.

Abe had just been hung up on again by Wilma. Every time he called it was the same. She said she would call him when she was ready, and for him not to call her in the meantime. If Rocky answered the phone he said the same thing then hung up.

He couldn't stand it much longer. He had promised not to drink and he had stayed sober for a few days after making the promise, but when she wouldn't even talk to him on the phone he decided that it served her right if he went ahead and drank. And drink he did. Even more than before. *It's all her fault, and I'm going to make sure I stay drunk as much as possible. There's no need to restrict myself now.*

I want my family back. Then I'll stop drinking. Everything will be just fine once they came to their senses and return to me. I'm the bread winner and the husband and the father. They need me, and I know it. They're just being stubborn and arrogant. Sooner or later they'll come crawling back. Then I'll have the upper hand again.

------- <◇> -------

Wilma was getting sick of the phone calls. She didn't want to ever talk to Abe again and had told him so. But he wouldn't listen and had begged and pleaded so she finally told him she'd think about it. She was so sorry she had given in to him even that little bit. Now she just wanted him gone out of her and Rocky's life forever. She had been considering telling him that Rocky wasn't his son, hoping that he would then leave them alone. But she couldn't be sure he wouldn't do something violent if she told him, so she hadn't decided what. Meanwhile, she wanted him to stop calling. Rocky had told her he felt the same way but was also still afraid of Abe and didn't know how to get him to leave them alone.

Wilma had been meeting her friend Nancy two or three times a week for coffee. She really needed the support her friend gave her, and they had started confiding more and more with each other. It was Nancy that suggested a restraining order against Abe. So Wilma had gone to the courthouse a few weeks before and started the process, but nothing would be final until Abe was served. She didn't know when that would happen, but expected it any day.

Getting Abe out of her life had taken on a new urgency recently. The last time she visited Clint he had asked her on a date. She remembered the conversation clearly. Her mind wandered back to that moment.

"I've been thinking a lot about you lately," he had said.

"You're just bored. You'd think a lot about Frankenstein if he came to visit you as often as I do," she replied.

"Maybe so. But you're prettier than he is. And I don't particularly want to take him out on a date."

There was a long silence while she just looked at him. She remembered feeling her cheeks turning red, bright red. But she didn't turn away. And she didn't tell him she had been thinking about a date also. In fact, thinking about him was what she had been doing most of the time. Still, a lady wouldn't let on to a fellow about such things. At least not yet.

Then she had a terrible thought. What if he wasn't asking her out on a date? Had she just jumped to a conclusion that she so wanted to jump to? He hadn't said he wanted to date her, just that he didn't want to date Frankenstein. Oh dear, she had thought, what do I say now?

Clint waited for her response. But when she silently sat there, with a red face, he hadn't known what to do next. Finally he said, "I guess I overstepped with that comment. Please forgive me."

"You didn't overstep," she quickly said.

"Then it's a date," he said, quick to take the opportunity while it was there. "Your next day off work is four days from now, on Friday. I'll make reservations for 6 pm at a nice restaurant, and I'll arrange a hotel room for you for that night so you won't have to drive home so late."

For the rest of their visit that day neither of them spoke about what had transpired. They were both nervous about it, and fearful that it had finally after so many years been put into words. Yet both of them were very excited that their relationship was going to move to another level. For Wilma it also represented the figurative end of her marriage to Abe.

------- <<>> -------

The sheriff had no sooner driven away on that Monday morning than Abe opened a bottle. *So now I can't go near my wife or son. How dare she serve me with a restraining order? At least it's not divorce papers. But we were supposed to work things out, weren't we? If must be that Clint Larkins guy. He's probably been putting a move on her to get her away from me. She's still ok looking, even at her age. Yep, that's it all right. He's trying to get her for himself. Betcha he's wooing Rocky too. What with that motorcycle and all. That son-of-a-bitch Larkins. The restraining order doesn't say I have to stay away from him. Tomorrow I'll go find him and teach him a lesson he won't forget. That sorry bastard.*

Two hours later when Abe went to work it was the first time he had ever shown up drunk. The Refinery had no patience with anyone drinking on the job, or coming to work after drinking. It was way too dangerous around all of the equipment for anyone to be impaired. They were even careful about prescription medications because so many of them made the person less alert.

Abe knew better. For many years he had been a drunk, but never in a way that would get him in trouble at work. He had always been able to maintain himself in that way. Until then, anyway. He probably didn't even feel it when the crane hook hit the side of his head. It was a big crane that they used to lift heavy equipment from one part of the Refinery to another. The spotter on the ground knew Abe was there, but he expected Abe to stay clear just like he always did. The crane operator couldn't even see that piece of ground from his perch up high where he relied on hand signals to tell him where to move the huge hook. The spotter was just starting to signal for the operator to do an emergency stop as Abe stepped right in front of the oncoming hook, but it was too late.

Wilma and Rocky didn't have much time together until Wednesday evening, two days after the accident at the Refinery. Neither of them had gone to see Abe in the hospital and as far as they knew he was still in a coma. Neither of them wanted much to do with the whole affair, but she felt that she owed it to her son, to say nothing of herself, for them to talk about it. She and Rocky had talked very briefly Monday evening, but both of them were somewhat devoid of emotion about Abe and his coma. Whatever emotions they would have normally had were overwhelmed by the horror of what he had recently done to both of them, and their memories of those events were still quite clear.

It seemed as if any love they used to have for Abe had disappeared under the pain of his brutality and drinking. Or perhaps the love had long ago dissipated into nothingness but neither of them had been able or willing to end their relationships with him. Whatever the reasons, what both of them felt certainly wasn't heartbreak. That night they sat up together and talked until early morning.

She told him about her telephone conversation with the human resources director at the Refinery, which had occurred that morning. She had been informed that Abe would be terminated for being intoxicated on the job, but owing to his many years of loyal service he wouldn't be fired until he awoke and was discharged from the hospital, if that should ever happen, so that his medical insurance would continue to cover his hospital stay. That also meant Abe's family's medical benefits would end when his employment ended.

So she was now concerned about losing medical insurance for her son and herself, along with all the other worries she had about money and providing a home for the two of them. After learning about Abe's future termination, she had spoken that morning with Mr. Zorn about the possibility of getting medical insurance through the Pharmacy and he told her he would look into that and some other matters involving her employment status. Meanwhile, he had told her, try not to worry about it all because he felt that it was all going to work out ok for her and Rocky.

Around 2 am on Thursday morning, having talked most of the night away, she told Rocky that Clint had asked her out to dinner. To her surprise, he was very happy about it, saying it seemed appropriate that his parents should go out together. She had dreaded that he would be upset and she didn't know how to deal with that, but she knew she had to tell him before Friday. If she didn't tell him, he would see that as a betrayal when he inevitably found out anyway.

The next day, Thursday, she went shopping during her split shift break and bought a new outfit for her date with Clint. But she couldn't help feeling a little sad about Abe, and wondered if she should cancel her upcoming date. He was, after all, still her husband. But she had been planning to divorce him anyway as soon as she could figure out how to do it without risking her or anyone else's safety. So now the jerk had gone and gotten himself into a coma making her decisions about a divorce even harder to figure out. Then she realized that she couldn't let him still interfere in her life. Just having to be concerned about her and others' safety regarding Abe was reason enough to not dwell on him anymore, coma or not. She was determined to not let him have any power over her anymore. It was time for her to have a life that she would treasure, not dread. Friday was going to be a watershed event in her life and she wasn't going to let Abe interfere with it, even if he was awake by then.

NINETEEN

Early Summer, 1999

"She's all ready for you. Brand new, gassed up and ready to go. She's sure a beauty, isn't she?" the salesman asked.

"Indeed she is," Clint replied. "And the paperwork?"

"Right there in the saddlebag. And the special license plate you wanted came in this morning so it's already mounted for you."

"Thanks again for your help in getting everything done so quickly. Especially with the DMV."

Clint sat on the gleaming machine, feeling somewhat out of place. He had sat on Teaser so many thousands of times, but this machine was shiny and new. Teaser was old and weather worn. But he loved Teaser like no other, and this new lady would have to prove herself to him. He wanted to give her every opportunity to live up to her predecessor's legacy. That's one reason he had ordered the personalized license plate for her, so she would feel a part of the family right from the start.

He knew she was already getting used to having him astride her so her inclusion into the family would surely go smoothly.

He held her two round, firm grips in his strong hands. He felt her against his buttocks and groin. He leaned back against her backrest and luxuriated in her welcoming embrace. And he felt how she was between his legs – all quiet at the moment but with a sense of great power and nimbleness. Ready to take him wherever he wanted her to go. Ready for his every command.

His love for Teaser, and for his dear, dear Meredith, the original teaser who had brought Teaser the motorcycle into his life, always contributed to his sensual feelings about what most people would consider just a steel and iron machine with some leather for comfort. And now he could feel some of that same love beginning to develop for this new steel and iron machine and its brand new leather.

I can hardly wait to show my new love to Rocky. What a surprise it'll be. Now we can ride together. Father and son. And Wilma too. I sure hope she's going to like riding with me, pressed up against my back. How I look forward to all that.

The salesman's query brought him back to the moment, interrupting a spiritual moment for the man who was winning against the cancer and who had been spending much of his time lately thinking about wooing a remarkable woman that he had wanted for such a long time.

"Is there anything else I can help you with?" the salesman asked.

"No thanks. I'll be on my way now."

But it took a few moments longer for Clint to come to grips with the fact that he wasn't going to have to kick start this beauty. Then, with a very strange feeling indeed, he pressed the thumb switch and the mighty roar brought a tear to his eyes. Pressing the shifter into 1st, he slowly released the clutch lever and he was off, leaving the Harley-Davidson dealership and the salesman behind in his thoughts.

He turned the handlebars towards Mill Mountain and headed towards that respite from the city that was so conveniently located in the middle of the Shenandoah Valley, right within Roanoke city itself. He had a couple of hours before needing to return for his very last chemotherapy treatment, and he wanted to feel the wind. And feel it he did. Such a wonderful, wonderful thing it was to experience the wind and temperature and sun and smells without being encapsulated inside a steel box on wheels. Feeling the mighty V-Twin rumbling between his legs chased away all thoughts of anything else, leaving only his body's sensations.

------- <<>> -------

Victor Zorn had driven his boss over to the motorcycle dealership that morning and dropped him off. Even though Clint had asked him not to come to Roanoke to see him, Victor had an important matter that he needed to discuss so they had met early that morning. Clint didn't want visitors while he was undergoing treatment, except for Wilma and Rocky. He welcomed their visits, although he tried to have them scheduled when he wasn't likely to feel bad following a treatment.

On that morning Victor had arranged a meeting because of a personal emergency. Clint had agreed to the meeting immediately upon being told it was an urgent personal matter even without knowing what it was. He had always been a compassionate boss, even during the many long years when he had been absent from the business and lived in a wood shack in the forest behind Fran's Fabrics. Mr. Zorn was such a good and self-sufficient manager for the Pharmacy that Clint's involvement was essentially nil, but upon a very few rare occasions Victor had left a note or question for Clint to see when he came by periodically at night to review the books. They had grown to know and respect each other during the time that Victor worked for Clint before he sank into despair and stopped coming to work. It was because of Clint's compassion as a person and a boss that Victor had tirelessly maintained the business while Clint wasn't able to do so.

During their meeting that morning Clint had agreed with everything Victor had asked about, which gave the manager a tremendous sense of relief. He had explained that his aging mother needed daily assistance so she could stay in her home, which she very much wanted to do. Victor's widowed sister lived with their mother and took care of the older woman, but she had to work three days a week. That hadn't been a problem until recently, and now his sister had asked Victor to help out during those three days each week.

Victor, who had never married, wanted to be able to reduce his work load to three days a week, thus allowing him travel time for the five-hour drive each way to his mother's home. He knew his pay would have to be reduced, but he really needed to change his schedule. Unfortunately that would leave the Pharmacy with only a part-time manager and no assistant manager available from the current regimen of full-time employees.

Then, to Victor's great excitement, Wilma had asked about medical insurance. Victor knew that she had managed the business years before when she worked for Clint, before Rocky was born. And during her time at the Pharmacy over the last few months while she worked a split shift her management ability had shown clearly. So Victor asked his boss if Wilma could be a full-time assistant manager and receive medical benefits as well.

Victor, in his complete honesty, also informed Clint that he felt unsure about having someone of personal interest to the owner acting in a managerial position because of potential problems that might occur. But his experience with Wilma was such that he felt like her and Clint's personal relationship would not interfere with her job.

Clint immediately agreed to everything his manager asked for, while reassuring him that Wilma's professionalism wouldn't be a worry at all. He also told Victor to adjust Wilma's salary to an appropriate amount for her new responsibilities. Besides, he thought to himself, if she's there full-time then he would have more opportunities to pursue a relationship with her.

Clint told Victor that his salary should remain unchanged for the time being, until they knew more about how much long-term care the elderly Mrs. Zorn would be needing.

During the drive from Clint's hospital to the motorcycle dealership, Victor brought his boss up to date on matters at the Pharmacy and around town, including Wilma's husband's accident and subsequent coma.

------- <<>> -------

Thursday night proved to be windy with downpours and frequent lightning. Fortunately the power stayed on. Wilma felt fatigued from having been up practically all night Wednesday while she and Rocky talked and talked, but even so sleep remained elusive for her.

So she turned on the light and retrieved one of Meredith's diaries from the closet and opened it at random. She read a paragraph or two, then opened to another page and read a bit there. She didn't know what she was looking for, but the mundane daily activities that Meredith often wrote about just weren't of interest to her in the midst of the noisy storm outside.

Then a passage really snapped her to attention. Clint had purchased an old car while dating Meredith, and she had written about one Saturday night after a movie. Wilma had learned enough about the young couple's time-line together to know that they had been doing a lot of petting by the time of that diary entry.

"Dear Diary. Tonight was really wonderful. Wonderful and scary. Clint took us to a movie but I can't even remember the name of it right now. So much happened afterwards. Oh Diary, how amazing it was!

"I knew something was up with Clint. He held me and kissed me all during the movie. You know he always does that, but this was, I don't know, different. He was more, I don't know. I guess the best word is intense. He was more intense than usual. But he wasn't pushing himself on me, he was just feeling it more, somehow. Anyway, it made me feel more intense too. When he kissed me and held my breast at first I felt soft and faint inside, but then I started getting real tense and anxious inside. My breath was coming much faster than other times when we've done that. He pulled his hand away when I shifted position to get closer to him, but then he didn't put it back.

"I always like it when he touches me, but tonight I was really wanting him to do it even more. We were both breathing hard and when he nibbled on my neck I grabbed his hand and held it to my breast! Dear Diary, I've never been so bold with him before! I don't know what came over me but I just really wanted to feel him holding me there. It was wonderful. So wonderful that my panties were getting wet. I was afraid it would soak through and wet my skirt! We were both breathing really fast. But he must have been holding back. I've felt him come enough times to know when it happens, and he seemed to be stopping it for some reason. I didn't know what was going on. He knows it's ok with me when it happens. So why was he holding back? He even pulled his hand away, and he's never done that before.

"Then he asked if we could leave the movie right then. I was still feeling hot and wanted to keep on, but he was insistent. So we left and he drove us to a dirt road just outside of town and parked. Then he asked me if we could please get in the back seat. We've done that a few times, and I know it always gets real hot for both of us. Since I was still hot I jumped right over into the back without even answering him.

"He was so surprised he didn't know what to say. I usually resist until he talks me into getting in back, and then only after getting him to promise that we won't do anything we shouldn't. But it only took him a moment to figure out that I didn't need convincing and he jumped over the seat faster than I've ever seen him do it before. I laughed when his foot got caught and he landed on his head. But that didn't stop him! He jumped right up and sat real close beside me and started kissing me again.

"It was wonderful. He held my breast and I got really turned on. I surprised myself at how intense and grownup I was feeling! Then his hand started moving down my side to my hip. I was breathing so fast I almost didn't even notice his hand, and when I did notice I didn't want him to stop. He paused. It seemed like forever. That boy just doesn't seem to know when he has permission and when he doesn't. All I could think about was how would it feel if he held me down there? If it felt like when he holds my breast, then I wanted him to get a move on. And if it felt even better, like when I touch myself, then he'd better really get a move on. I was really turned on and he wasn't moving.

"Remember, Dear Diary, how I learned so much from my cousins and the ranch hands at my uncle's farm during the summers I spent there? How they bragged about doing it with girls? Remember they all liked to drink too much around the campfire on Saturday nights and I'd pretend to have fallen asleep and then they talked and bragged with each other as if I wasn't even there? That sure taught me a lot about you know what. And seeing the horses and other animals jumping on each other was weird at first but interesting too.

"So I figure I must know more about it than Clint does. That makes me feel older or something. Better, maybe? I don't know. But I do know I wanted my guy to do some of the things my cousins and the other guys always talked so much about. Not all of it of course. Just some of it. And soon!"

Wilma held the diary with one hand and started moving her other hand down to touch herself. It had been holding her breast and she realized that she was breathing hard. But then she thought that it would be more intense if she waited to touch herself until Meredith was being touched by Clint. She held her hand on the side of her hip, waiting, wanting, and breathing hard.

"I nudged his arm with my elbow. Get moving, fella! Sometimes that guy is hard headed. If he didn't do it soon I was gonna have to touch myself. My whole insides were shaking around so much he must have felt it. I leaned over and started biting his neck. You'd think that would get him moving, but no.

"I couldn't stand it another second. That guy needs help! I took his hand and put it right between my legs. I don't know if he was shocked or not. I couldn't tell because as soon as I pressed his hand against me I started to come and forgot about him. Except for his hand, that is. I've never come so hard in all my life! He had never felt me come but I think he knew what was happening because he held me real tight and kept kissing my ear and kept pressing his hand against me and squeezing. That was the most remarkable sexual experience ever. I can't wait until we can do that again!"

Wilma's right hand went straight to her clitoris and her spasms were as powerful as she had ever felt. The diary fell from her other hand, which then went immediately to her right breast and started caressing her hard nipple until it hurt. She barely suppressed a huge scream, but instead moaned loud and long. The thunder outside and the driving rain against the roof muffled her noises so Rocky wouldn't hear her. Or so she hoped and prayed.

The spasms kept on coming, and she was panting so hard she thought she'd die. But even with the thought of a suffocating death she couldn't stop rubbing herself and her nipple.

After what seemed like a really long time her body relaxed from its spasmodic tightness and she retrieved the diary from the floor and quickly found the page to continue with Meredith's story.

"But that's not all, Dear Diary. That wonderful man held me until I was completely done, but then I realized that he was shaking and panting. He hadn't come yet! He reached his other hand to my breast and held me in both of the places that must have been really important to him while he kept shaking. But he still wasn't coming! After what he had done for me I knew I had to do something really marvelous for him. So I reached over and touched him. Right on his thing!

"Oh Diary, that sent him wild! I'd never touched him there, even though I'd felt it against me when we slow danced. It felt amazing. Long and so hard. His pants were damp. I guess he's like me and gets moist before he comes. He put his hand over mine and pressed it even harder against his thing and started moving my hand back and forth. He was shaking all over and I could feel him throbbing under my hand. I guess he felt really bold because he really shocked me with what he did next. Not shocked bad, shocked good. Actually, shocked great!

"He somehow got his pants unzipped and pulled himself out and put my hand right around him!!!! What a feeling I had! I can't describe it. It was so wonderful to hold my man that way. To feel him jump at my touch. I felt powerful and romantic and sexy all at the same time! It was kinda wet and sticky and I think he might have used some saliva to wet it more but I'm not sure. I know that sounds icky but it was really exciting. He kept his hand over mine and moved my hand up and down until I got the hang of it. Then he went back to my breast. There we were with one of his hands on my breast, one between my legs, and me rubbing him! When he came it squirted all over my hand and arm and all over his pants and even the back of the front seat. And it had a smell that I've never known before. I don't know if I liked the smell or not, but it wasn't bad. Just different.

"It must have taken him 10 minutes to stop jerking in my hand and to stop shaking all over. He likes to call me his teaser. I sure didn't tease him tonight!

"Now, Dear Diary, I'm just plumb worn out. I betcha Clint is all worn out too! He sure was happy when he headed home. But I'm still tingly all over so I think I'll touch myself until I fall asleep. I just know I'll dream about him all night long."

Wilma had another orgasm while reading the rest of Meredith's passage. The thought of having Clint with her in the back seat of a car felt extremely powerful. It was also quite interesting, she thought, that she identified so closely with Meredith while reading the diary. Each time she read another diary entry, she realized how similar they were in so many ways. Wilma could easily picture herself as a teenager, and, had she been in love with a nice boy, doing and saying the same things that Meredith had said and done. She wondered if Clint saw similarities between them also.

At that moment she realized, again, how much she loved him, and how much she wanted to be with him always. She put the diary on the side table, switched off the light, and resolved to do the same thing Meredith had done while falling asleep. Outside the storm let up and it started clearing towards what was going to be a wonderful morning.

TWENTY

"Where the hell am I?" he said aloud, feeling disoriented and afraid.

Why am I so groggy? And why does everything look hazy and weird? Where the hell am I? Are those tubes stuck in my arm? Where am I? I'm in a bed. Is this a hospital? How the hell did I get here? Where am I? Oh God my head hurts. Where am I?

Really scared by then, he shouted, "WHERE THE HELL AM I?"

There's a big woman coming over. Man, she's big. Who is she? She's wearing white. Am I in a hospital?

"Well now, I see you be waking, Mr. Powlison," the nurse's aide said. "Jes you relax and I'll call Doctor. Don't be movin' round jes yet. You be needin' to go slow at first. I'll go call Doctor. You jes stay calm now, ya hear? Back in a jiffy." She was gone before he could ask her any questions.

What's wrong with me? I'm so groggy. Why can't I see better? How'd I get here? Why the hell does my head hurt like hellfire? I can't hardly think straight what with the pain. What the hell's goin on here?

Wilma! It must've been because of Wilma. Yeah, I remember bein pissed at Wilma. Really pissed. Now I remember, she got a restraining order. That bitch. How could she do that to me? That total bitch. It must be her fault I'm here. But what the hell happened?

How'd I end up here in this place? Must be a hospital. Why does my head hurt like it's stuck in a vise? Where was I? Oh yeah. I was at work and the crane hook came right at me. If Wilma hadn't pulled that shit on me I'd have seen it comin like I always do. That bitch. This is her fault. All hers. I need to teach her somethin about bein a wife. Got a restraining order against me, did she? Well, that ain't gonna stop you from gettin one hell of a beatin, you whore. You'll see who wears the pants around here you dumb broad.

Gotta get up and go find the bitch. Why can't I sit up? WHY CAN'T I SIT UP? Damn, that sure hurts my head. What the hell's wrong? And where the hell am I?

Wait a minute. That son-of-a-bitch Larkins has been puttin a move on Wilma. And I bet he's been tryin to get Rocky away from me. Guess I need to teach him somethin too. With him I won't hold back either. He's goin down. Soon's I get my hands on that bastard he's goin down hard. I'm gonna finish him off good. Bet he put her up to that restraining order. It's his fault too what happened to me at work. I think I'll finish him off first. Then I can tell the bitch what I did to him while I'm teachin her some respect. I gotta get outta here right now.

"You be still now, Mr. Powlison," the nurse's aide said while entering the room. "We got you strapped down. Don't want you a fallin' outta bed. Jes relax. Doctor be here in a minute. HOLD STILL!"

"Where the hell am I?" he demanded.

"You in hospital. Take a nasty blow aside your head, you did. They said it be a crane hook what got ya. Got ya pretty good, too. You been out cold. Couple days now. Doctor sewed you up real purty, but you be havin' headache for awhile. Probably a whopper at that."

"I gotta get outta here," he said, barely able to see the large woman. "Untie me right now. And get me some pain pills. Feels like a car ran over my head. Untie me."

"Now you jes hold still. You ain't going no place till Doctor sees ya. He be along afore ya knows it. Hold still or you pull them stitches loose. Then you be in pickle all over again. I SAID HOLD STILL!"

"Where the hell am I?"

"I already told ya. You in hospital. You done cracked yer head purty good. Lay still and soon's Doctor sees ya he order pain pills."

"Why can't I see you better? You're all smeary looking."

"That crane smack ya up good. They was able to save you sight but maybe not all the way. Not right away, fo sure. Maybe it git better, they said. Doctor tell you more. I not supposed tell ya much of nothin'. Doctor the boss, ya know."

"Yeah yeah. Tell him to hurry it up."

The aide left the room without responding to him.

------- <<>> -------

Wilma parked her car and excitedly headed for Clint's room. She wore her brand new dress, deep blue with light blue trim around the bodice. It was long and flowed like a gentle breeze when she walked. It fit her slim figure just right and flattered her like a princess. She would have never spent so much on herself, but this was the most important date she had ever been on in her entire life.

Her brand new shiny black high heels clicked on the floor in the hallway. She liked the sound, it made her feel feminine and sexy. She wore her favorite sapphire stud earrings and a small, elegant sapphire necklace. Her small black handbag completed the ensemble.

She paused in front of a mirror in the hallway and checked her dark brown hair and makeup. All perfect, she decided, and continued to Clint's room. His door was open and she stood just inside the room and waited quietly for just a few moments until he felt her standing there.

"Beautiful," he said, "absolutely beautiful. I've never seen you so dressed up and you look wonderful."

"Thank you. You're looking pretty great yourself," she said, noticing his suit and how he had selected a tie and shirt that enhanced his good looks. *What a change from how you've been for so many years. What a miraculous change. Whatever you have planned for tonight, the answer is yes.*

"Well come on in and let's chat a few minutes. We'll need to leave in 20 minutes or so for dinner. Sit down. I can offer you water or soda. Actually I have both chilled water and room temperature. No alcohol, though. They won't even let me have a beer."

"I'm fine thanks. Where are you taking us for dinner?"

------- <<>> -------

Rocky wished his mom well just as she was leaving their apartment. He had some strange feelings about her going on a date with Clint. Even more so since it was sort of an overnight date, even though she had told him she was staying over in a hotel and not with Clint. He had only known Abe as his dad until recently when she told him that 'Uncle' Clint was his real father. Since then he had visited to Roanoke several times, and had talked some with Clint about why hadn't he come forward himself to tell Rocky the truth years ago.

Clint had explained that he hadn't known at first that he was his father, having only discovered the truth when Rocky was a child and his doctor sent in some blood tests because the boy was ill. At that time practically all lab work for the community was processed through Gold's Pharmacy and Clint had seen Rocky's blood type. Since he already had Abe's and Wilma's blood types in his files, he knew Abe wasn't the father. And just by looking at Rocky it was easy to see the resemblance to his real father, both with blond hair and quite similar features.

He went on to explain that Wilma had never left Abe, and seemed determined to make her marriage work. It would have been wrong, Clint said, for him to come forward then. So he trusted that Wilma would make the right decisions regarding how to care for Rocky.

But the most important thing Clint said to Rocky was that he had always loved him, and now that the truth was out he hoped they could have a relationship based on love and trust. Rocky agreed that he would like that, and so ended the conversation about paternity.

On that Friday afternoon, with Mom going to Roanoke for a date with his dad, Rocky felt as if a ride on Teaser would help clear him of all the strange thoughts and emotions he was having. It would also keep him from thinking about what it might be like if Mom and Clint got together. He didn't want to ever even see Abe again, but he wasn't comfortable yet thinking of Clint as his dad.

He started the iron lady with only a couple of kicks. He had dedicated himself to learning how to start her easily. He had made that commitment to himself out of necessity. It she was recalcitrant about starting then he would end up with sore muscles all over. By following the advice from Clint, including several conversations on the subject since Clint had been in the hospital, he had managed to achieve a fairly consistent pattern of getting her started with only two or three lunges. Each lunge had to have his entire weight and complete concentration behind it, but it was well worth it. The alternative was pain, frustration, and a motorcycle that teased him instead of starting.

He never needed much of an excuse to jump on Teaser for a ride, and this afternoon the weather was perfect and she seemed to beckon him. With his mom gone until the next day he wouldn't even have to be back for dinner.

So off he headed, going west towards the Blue Ridge Parkway. He enjoyed riding anywhere at all, and had a special desire to try more of the twisty mountain road that he had only briefly sampled so far. Just before starting up into the mountains he stopped for gas at Beckett's Market and Gas. He had never stopped there before and didn't know what to expect inside.

After the attendant filled Teaser's gas tank Rocky went inside to pay and grab something that he could eat quickly before riding up into the mountains. That usually meant a bag of pretzels, so he looked around the store to find them. His attention was on his search when he noticed some hand-made sandwiches near the small grill in the market, including some peanut butter and jelly. His mom used to fix PB&J sandwiches for him frequently, and he was missing her that afternoon, so he grabbed two of them, forgetting about pretzels, and turned to go to the checkout counter.

He turned so quickly that he bumped smack into the tall, skinny, tomboy of a girl that had come up behind him with a handful of items to stock onto the shelves. The merchandise went flying but neither of them was hurt. "That your cycle?" she asked, smiling at him.

"Yeah," he said, wondering why he had just sounded so stupid with his one syllable of an answer.

Rocky was a good looking teen, with blond hair, a good build, a quick smile that could be quite disarming, and a friendly nature. But he was a bit awkward and unsure of himself around girls and hadn't dated more than a couple of times until he got Teaser. He had often tried to socialize with girls at school but it always ended with him feeling and acting stupid, just like today.

But then Teaser came into his life. From the day he had purchased her, his confidence had taken a great leap. He felt like a young man now instead of an awkward adolescent. And many of the girls were really impressed with his motorcycle and had asked for rides. Since he started riding her to school his dating life had begun to blossom. He still felt awkward around girls but didn't feel stupid anymore, and he had already been out with several different ones on Teaser.

He liked to go out on dates, but his awkwardness still got in the way frequently. He just didn't yet know how to get past the first or second date with a girl. But that was ok with him because he didn't really know any girls that he thought of as a possible steady. There were several that he would like to go out with, but not to go steady with.

So it was quite a surprise to him how his emotions soared the moment he saw this particular girl. Not only that, but his recently mature demeanor had just flown the coop and left him not knowing what to say or do next. He was quite confused at the whole situation.

"It's nice," she said.

"Yeah." There it was again, he thought. Stupid.

"You ever take anyone for a ride?" she asked.

"No."

She waited a moment longer, then turned around and walked away without even picking up the dropped bread and boxes she had been carrying.

Why had he said that? Of course he had taken girls for rides. How stupid could he get?

He didn't know what was going on. He didn't lie to girls, yet he had outright lied to this one. And he had acted really, really stupid, just like he used to around girls before, especially the pretty ones. And this girl wasn't even pretty. Cute, in a tomboyish way, but not blond cheerleader pretty. Why had he acted like such a dunce? And now she was leaving him just standing there. Not that he deserved any better, but he knew something wasn't right. He wanted to know more about her, but how? She probably wouldn't give him the time of day after that.

"But I'd like to," he said. He didn't know where that had come from. His conscious thoughts were confused and still very busy telling himself how stupid he had been. But somehow his higher self had managed to at least try to save the day on his behalf.

She returned and started picking up the merchandise, with his help. "My parents would kill me if I just rode off with a stranger," she said. "What's your name?"

"I'm Rocky. Rocky Powlison. What's yours?

"Samantha Tanner. But my friends call me Sami."

"Hi Sami. I'd really like to give you a ride on Teaser." He was recovering a bit now, and felt like he could talk a little better. But his insides were still in turmoil. A lot of turmoil.

"Is that what you call it? Teaser? Why?"

"That's a long story. Maybe we can sit somewhere together and I'll tell you about her."

"I get off in a few minutes. How about if we sit on the old log next to the store. Are you in a hurry to leave?"

"No hurry. I'll be there." His highly anticipated ride up into the mountains was suddenly not important, and he hoped to find out more about this girl that had set his insides into a mess. He went and paid his bill, then moved Teaser to the side of the store where he saw a large log that someone had added a backrest to. When he got to it he saw that the top had been worn smooth from many years as a local sitting place. He sat down and waited for Sami, wondering why she had had such an impact on him.

"When do you think you'll be leaving here?" Wilma asked. They were walking to her car, then they would be going to dinner at a restaurant Clint had picked out for them.

"Tomorrow. The doctor came by this afternoon and gave me the ok to leave. I told the staff I'd check out tomorrow."

"Oh, that's wonderful! I'm so happy for you! I'm so happy that you're all better. I don't want to lose you." That last comment had slipped out before she could stop herself. She didn't want to put any pressure on him, even though she had already decided she wanted him completely. But she didn't know enough yet about what he wanted.

"I don't want to lose you either," he said.

They were both silent, not knowing how to continue from there. For all their years of life's experience, they were both naïve when it came to dating.

Then she suddenly realized that she and Rocky were staying in Clint's apartment and he would be needing it. She felt horrified that she hadn't thought of that before. It wasn't like her to be so thoughtless. "Oh dear," she said, reaching over and holding Clint's arm, "you'll be needing your apartment. I should have thought of it sooner. Rocky and I will move out tomorrow. Oh Clint, I'm so sorry I was thoughtless and didn't bring it up before."

"I've arranged to stay with Victor Zorn for a few days," he said, "while I figure out what to do. I want you and Rocky to stay in your apartment for just as long as you need it. You are not to leave on my account. Absolutely not. I'll be just fine, and there's no reason for you to be hard on yourself. You've had a lot on your mind lately and I want the two of you to know that you have a safe place to stay. A safe place for years to come."

"Oh Clint. You're so special. How can I thank you for all you've done for Rocky and me? We would have been in such a pickle without your generosity."

"It's all been my pleasure. You don't owe me anything."

She reached over and hugged him while kissing him on the cheek. She lingered a moment, holding him, then reluctantly let go. They had just gotten to the parking lot and were heading towards her car.

"Let me take you back to Johnson's Crossing tomorrow. It will be my pleasure to help you in every way I can," she said.

"I appreciate that, and I do want some help with my things, but there's something I want to show you. It's just over here." He turned her to walk across the parking area to the surprise.

As soon as she had been pointed in a new direction she immediately saw it. Just across the lot, sitting there all shiny, was a brand new motorcycle. It just had to be his. "Oh Clint, is that yours?" she asked.

"Take a look at the license plate," he said.

She went around to where she could see it. It said "TEASER 2".

TWENTY-ONE

By the time Sami joined Rocky outside Beckett's Market and Gas, he had already jumped up and walked around several times to relieve his anxiety. He kept wondering what his problem was. He didn't want to act stupid again, but he felt quite anxious and not at all sure about what he could say to the girl.

Fortunately for him, Sami started right in telling him about where she had gone to school and how she worked some afternoons and weekends at the market. But she didn't share any other information about herself, and when she asked him to tell her about himself he could barely muster anything to say. But he started to loosen up after a few exchanges. That was fortunate, because Sami had previously decided she would start the conversation but then if he couldn't get into it she would just leave and go home.

They talked for the better part of an hour, getting to know each other. He was feeling much more comfortable being with her, and his earlier inability to converse had passed completely away.

She felt comfortable enough with him by then to ask, "Want to walk me home and meet my parents?"

"I'll drive you. You said you wanted a ride on Teaser."

"Yeah I do, but not until after you meet Mom and Dad. So, walk me home?"

"Sure," he said, then added, "I'd love to."

"Come on," she said.

They walked for a couple of blocks, while she told him that her dad worked at Johnson's Refinery and had just been promoted. Since he would be working longer hours, he needed to move the family to Johnson's Crossing that summer so he would have a shorter commute. That meant Sami would be going to Rocky's high school next fall for her senior year. His heart leaped at that news and he reached out without thinking and took her hand in his.

She stopped dead in her tracks and looked straight into his eyes, which were at about the same level as hers. But she didn't pull her hand away. She just looked deeply into him, as if looking at his soul. The old Rocky would have pulled back and looked away, but the new Rocky with his confidence somewhat restored from earlier in the afternoon stood his ground and looked right back into her eyes. He didn't know what he was looking for, nor what she was looking for, but he felt that he needed to be open to her unspoken inquiry.

Then, without a word, she started walking again. She held onto his hand.

"Oh darn it," she said abruptly.

"What's wrong?"

"My brothers are in the driveway playing basketball. See? Down there on the right? I had hoped they would be off somewhere. Listen, just walk with me and we're going straight into the house. But I don't want them to see you holding my hand. Don't even look over at them and maybe we can get by without being noticed."

He felt some fear in his chest and stomach. There were four guys playing ball and they all looked older and bigger. He knew how possessive some guys were about their sisters, and here were four of them. He didn't like how this was going. But he stayed beside Sami as she picked up the pace, and he didn't look over at them, just as she had directed.

It didn't work. They saw the couple and all turned to stare. Rocky could see them out of the corner of his eyes, all the while getting more scared by the minute. But the guys didn't say anything and stayed where they were. Sami kept up a fast pace and they went past the driveway, then up the walk and in the door.

Sami greeted the woman that was just coming from the kitchen towards the front door with a cheery, "Hi Mom."

The moment he knew they were in the mother's presence his insides relaxed noticeably. He didn't think he was in any imminent danger so long as he stayed near the woman. Any jitters he had been feeling before about meeting Sami's parents were gone and replaced by a great sense of relief. He thought that he would never again be nervous to meet a girl's parents.

After introductions they went to the kitchen table and Mrs. Tanner produced some cookies while they sat and talked. She was a friendly, happy person and made him feel at ease immediately. She was also adept at finding out about him without it seeming like an interview. Sami had seen her mother do this many times before, but usually with one of her brothers' friends, not hers. So she knew the process and also knew she had to be patient until her mom was satisfied and showed that she approved of Rocky. Only then did Sami ask if it would be ok if she took a ride with Rocky on his motorcycle. Mrs. Tanner's concern that her daughter must wear a helmet was put to rest when Rocky assured her that he had an extra one.

Mrs. Tanner excused herself from the conversation to attend to something else, leaving the new couple alone. Sami took him to the living room where they sat in separate chairs, and she asked, "So when do I get that ride?"

"How's tomorrow morning at 10?" he asked. "We can go up to the Blue Ridge Parkway. Oh, you know what? We could even do a picnic!"

His enthusiasm pleased her. Actually, everything about him pleased her. Once he had gotten over his shyness he seemed to her a very likable boy. After they finalized the plans, with Sami offering that her mom would be happy to pack them a lunch, he got up to leave. She walked to the door with him, then remembered her two brothers and their friends in the driveway.

"I'll get Mom to go outside and keep those guys from bothering you while you leave. Then tonight I'll threaten them with a gruesome death if they bother you tomorrow when you come over. Wait here a minute."

She left the living room in search of her mom, then returned a couple of minutes later and said, "Mom's on her way outside. I had a really nice time with you today. See ya tomorrow." She took his hand and squeezed it for a moment.

"Me too. Bye now," he said, and began tentatively moving through the front door. Once he saw that Mrs. Tanner had reached the young men in the driveway he rapidly walked to the street then turned towards where Teaser awaited him. As soon as he was safely down the street he slowed his pace and smiled broadly. That Sami was quite a girl, he thought, while smiling even more broadly.

------- <<>> -------

Saturday morning arrived with brilliant sunshine and a grand blue sky. The air felt crisp and clean smelling. It was a perfect beginning to what would surely be a perfect day, Wilma thought.

She opened the window of her hotel room and breathed in the morning air, thinking how it was a perfect day for her man to go home. Home, of course, was actually the spare room at Mr. Zorn's house. But that didn't dim her romantic and adventurous thoughts about "her" man.

Their date the night before had been wonderful. Dinner at a very nice restaurant, then a drive up to Mill Mountain and a moonlit stroll beneath the Roanoke Star and on along a path through the trees. Once they were away from the Star's many lights, the glow coming up from the city was dim enough to allow the stars to shine brightly for the hand-holding couple. They sat on some boulders and just watched the sky and the city for an hour, talking and laughing.

He had told her how fond he was of that place, how he used to go there often starting back in 1949 when the Star was being constructed. At 100 feet high and made of steel girders in the shape of a star it had immediately become a big attraction throughout the Shenandoah Valley. He explained that it was the world's largest man-made star and symbolized Roanoke as the Star City of the South. It was high up on Mill Mountain and could be seen from many miles around. She knew he would have been there with Meredith and that's probably what made the place so special for him, but she didn't say anything. She had been very happy that he felt comfortable in bringing her to the place that used to be special with Meredith, and hoped that now it could be special for him with her.

On the way back to her car, Clint had taken her in his arms and kissed her gently on her willing lips. They stayed in each other's embrace for a long time while he kissed her cheeks, her eyes, then her ears and finally her neck. She couldn't remember having ever felt so romantic, so loved and cherished. She was almost limp in his arms, giving herself completely to the wonderful moment.

When he had finally pulled away he asked her if he was too old for her to have a long-term interest in. She was quite pleased at his question because of what it said about his desires and intentions towards her. She quickly assured him that their age difference was of no concern to her, and inquired if he was ok with it. His answer came as a kiss, this time allowing his tongue to gently explore hers.

When they finally reached her car she told him she had promised Rocky that Clint would not be staying with her that night, so he wouldn't be able to go back to her hotel room with her. His response was that Rocky's feelings about the two of them were very important to him also.

He did accompany her to the hotel and then took a taxi back to his private hospital room. They had arranged for her to come to the hospital the next morning to have breakfast together, then he would check out and ride Teaser 2 back to Johnson's Crossing.

In her mind he would be riding not to Johnson's Crossing, but instead to a new life with her and their son.

------- <<>> -------

Rocky awoke long before the alarm clock blared its intrusion. He arose and fixed himself a quick cereal, milk, and bagel breakfast. The sun was barely showing a sliver of a crescent above the horizon when he went outside in the crisp morning air to wash and dry Teaser so she would be ready for his date with the tomboyish girl that had so intrigued him the afternoon before. He was always nervous before a date, but this time felt different. His few dates had all been fun but Sami was different from the other girls he knew. She was special, although he didn't know how to describe what he felt. He just knew the feeling was different, and he liked it even though it made him nervous.

He grabbed some apples and bananas so he wouldn't show up empty handed, left a note for his mom, and took off for Sami's house. She lived a half hour away, at least until she moved to Johnson's Crossing, but a half hour on Teaser was always fun for Rocky so he didn't mind the distance at all.

As he neared her house he suddenly remembered her two brothers and how she had been concerned about them seeing the couple together. He hoped she had been able to convince them not to bother him, not just because he was afraid of them but especially since he didn't want anything to interfere between him and Sami. He decided to park Teaser on the street in front of her house instead of in her driveway just because it seemed more likely that he could avoid them that way.

No sooner had he shut off Teaser's rumbling engine than Sami came out of the house to greet him. She wore a boy's shirt with her jeans, but that looked sexy to Rocky even though it was nothing like what the other girls he knew would wear. She had a big smile for him and when she got to the street beside him and Teaser she reached over and took his hand in both of hers and squeezed for a moment before releasing him.

"I killed my brothers last night so they won't bother us," she said. "My dad's at work, but Mom wants to see your motorcycle and the extra helmet for me. Oh, here she comes now."

He laughed at the comment about her brothers. It was a nervous laugh, to be sure, but it did relax him a good bit.

After Mrs. Tanner joined them and they finished exchanging pleasantries and viewing Teaser and

Rocky's extra helmet, they went inside to gather up the picnic lunch Mrs. Tanner had prepared that morning. Then, as soon as the food was secured in a saddlebag, they were off.

------- <◇> -------

Mrs. Tanner watched from the front porch as they rode off. She wasn't at all happy about her daughter going off on a motorcycle, even with the helmet that Rocky had provided. She liked Rocky, so it wasn't about him. She just didn't want anything to happen to her daughter. But she kept her feelings to herself because she didn't want to discourage any rare bit of feminine behavior Sami displayed.

She had never seen her only daughter so happy to be going on a date. Usually it seemed to her as if Sami was only going out with a boy just to please her, not because the girl particularly wanted to. But this time was very different, and she felt really happy that Sami actually wanted to do something with a boy besides play sports. She decided it was time to try yet again to get Sami to wear some blouses instead of her brother's shirts that she always swiped from their room.

TWENTY-TWO

That son-of-a-bitch. How dare he come in here in the hospital and tell me I'll be fired. Manager of personnel, he calls himself. Manager of sorry-ass, that's what he is.

Here I am laid up cause of doing my job. That high falutin jerk with his suit and fancy tie. And tellin me how nice he's bein to not fire me till I'm outta the hospital. And take away my family's benefits too. I would of decked the fucker right here if I coulda seen him better. I can't even see right and they're firing me. I gave that fuckin company years of my sweat.

So what if I was high one time. I worked there my whole life and one lousy fuckin time I show up after a couple of drinks. That stupid asshole crane spotter screwed up and put me in this mess.

But it's really Wilma's fault. She made me so damn mad with that restrainin order. Tryin to keep me away from my family. Away from my son. No way am I stayin away from my family. Why the hell'd she do that anyway? So I got a couple too many drinks in me and smacked her and Rocky a couple times. They deserved it. A man's got a right to be boss in his own fuckin house, don't he? One time I show up a little high and they fire me. Those sorry bastards.

I gotta get outta here. Wilma's gonna pay, that bitch. And that old fart, what's his name? Oh yeah, Larkins. He's probably suckin up to her and Rocky right now while I'm not there to look after what's mine. That bastard. He's goin down. He's goin down hard.

I've worked for my family all these years and now they slap me with that damn restrainin order. Everything I've done it's been for them. Not that they've ever appreciated it.

That bitch needs a lesson right now. I'm gonna go find her. She needs to learn some respect for her husband. Then I'll go see the union boss and get my fuckin job back. They can't fire me. I'm union. But right now I'm gettin the hell outta here.

------- <<>> -------

Clint had ridden Teaser 2 back from Roanoke, with Wilma following in her car. It was an uneventful trip, except for her excitement at the whole situation. She wanted her new life with Clint to start immediately, but she knew they needed to evolve together some more first.

They drove straight to Victor Zorn's house and Clint found the door key hidden right where Victor had said it would be. Victor had left it there because he was away taking care of his elderly mother. Together they carried Clint's belongings to the spare room.

"This is a pleasant enough room," she said. "But if you'd like we can go shopping together and make it even more pleasant for you."

"I'd like that, but it's Victor's house and I wouldn't feel right putting things on the walls." He had no idea how to change the appearance of a room. And in this case he didn't see that it needed changing. It seemed a likable enough room. But the idea of Wilma wanting to make it nicer for him was very pleasing.

"We can do a lot with some nice accessories," she said.

"Do you have time right now?"

"Sure do. We should take my car. Teaser 2 doesn't have enough room to carry much back with us."

"Well then, let's go. I'd like your help in picking out some clothes too if you don't mind."

"Oh how wonderful! I'd love to clothes shop with you," she said, while leading the way to the front door.

Rocky was in heaven with Sami holding on behind him as he took the twisty road up to the Blue Ridge Parkway. She had her arms around him, and even though she wasn't pressed up against his back he could still feel her presence and every time he slowed it forced her forward against him. Even though she always pulled back a bit, he could still feel her arms around him and her thighs pressed against the outsides of his hips. Just having her with him felt wonderful.

When they reached the Parkway he turned Teaser north to follow it a ways. It was cooler up in the mountains and he felt a chill as the air whipped into his chest. He was glad to be protecting Sami from the full force of the cool wind. When he saw a turn to an overlook he followed that short road, planning to stop at the overlook and see if she was getting too cold. He had a couple of sweaters in the saddlebag that were going to come in handy while they rode.

They dismounted from Teaser in the small parking lot.

"Are you cold?" he asked.

"Yeah, a little. The air right here doesn't feel so cold, but riding along it sure did. That was fun. Are we staying here or going further?"

He could tell from her tone that she really wanted to go further, which was fine with him also. "Further is good. But I thought you might want a sweater first." He opened the saddlebag and handed her the nicer of the two sweaters.

"Oh, you're so sweet," she said, taking the sweater and putting it on. "Let's go see the overlook before riding further, ok?"

"Sure. I think there's a trail over there. Let's go."

After a few steps he took her hand in his and was very pleased that she accepted the gesture without hesitation. He led the way down the trail to the overlook. When they reached it they saw an old rusty railing at the far edge of the flattened out area, all of which seemed to teeter out over the sheer drop the mountain took down into the valley far below. They went to the railing and stood there for a few minutes enjoying the expansive view of the Shenandoah Valley.

The valley below them seemed a hodgepodge of family farms, small towns, roadways, and of course Roanoke, all interspersed with what was once a vast forest. Ample rainfall kept everything green during the growing season. From their vantage point cars and trucks looked like ants crawling ever so slowly along the ribbons of black. Surrounded by mountains that were lovely even if not majestic, the valley seemed serene and peaceful.

"Oh look, we can see the blue air today!" she said, referring to the blue haze that hung above the forested mountains. "There's no wind so it stays there."

"Yeah, it's great. Someone told me it's from oil in the tree leaves that evaporates and turns blue."

"It's fun to see."

Rocky held onto her hand the whole time, hoping that she liked that as much as he did. After a few minutes they returned to Teaser to ride further along the mountain peaks of the Blue Ridge Mountains.

Abe pulled the needle out of his arm, ignoring the blood that oozed copiously from where the needle had been. He jumped out of bed and immediately fell right over, dizzy from standing up so suddenly. As soon as he was able to stand he went to the small closet in the corner and found that his clothes were inside. He quickly changed then managed to exit the hospital without being recognized as a patient by anyone on the staff. There was a cab waiting at the door for someone else, but he jumped in and gave the driver his home address.

Before the cab stopped in front of the house he could see that Wilma's car wasn't there even with his hazy and limited eyesight. So he quickly went inside and grabbed a whiskey bottle before returning to the cab. Once he had his whiskey supply he directed the driver to go up and back through the town's streets. He spotted Wilma's car and a motorcycle after just a few minutes of looking. They were parked together in front of a house. He paid the driver and exited the cab a few doors down the street from where her car was parked.

He walked right up into the front yard without being seen, and hid behind some bushes that bordered the sidewalk and steps leading up to the porch. He planned to wait there until Wilma or Clint came out, then he would jump up and take whoever it was by surprise. He finished off the whiskey.

He hoped that Clint would be the first one that came down the steps. His anger grew by the moment, along with his intoxication. Pretty soon he started wondering what they were doing in there. Had she sunk so low that she'd do him right in there? What else would be keeping her? The longer he waited, the more he was determined to teach her a real lesson and to put the older man down completely.

He had grown tired of waiting and was about to go bang on the door when he heard voices and the screen door slammed. He peeked through the bushes and saw them coming down the steps. He could make out that it was Wilma in the lead. He planned to wait until they had both passed him by before leaping out behind them.

Wilma felt as happy as happy could be. Her new beau, or at least she hoped he was indeed her beau, wanted her to spend the afternoon with him while they shopped. It was wonderful to have him back from the hospital, and she hoped their relationship would move quickly. She didn't want to lose any more time waiting around.

Her son seemed to be gradually accepting Clint as his father, although she knew that would take some more time. But at least there didn't appear to be any real anger in Rocky about her and Clint being together. She was ever so thankful for that. And now both of the men she loved had motorcycles, so she hoped that would be a real unifying bond between them.

The future looked bright and happy for Wilma. She was absolutely delighted with how it was going, and right then felt really excited to be going shopping with her man. She almost broke into tears just thinking about it all while they traversed the porch steps and walked down the sidewalk towards her car. Then, out of nowhere, her reverie was shattered by a familiar, angry and drunk voice that came from just behind them.

"So there you are you bastard," Abe said while advancing menacingly towards Clint. "I knew you was trying to get Wilma away from me. Now you're gonna pay you fuckin' asshole. Now you're gonna pay good. Come here."

"How did you get here?" Wilma yelled. "You were unconscious. How did you get here? Are you drunk? You leave us alone!"

"Shut up, bitch. I'll get to you in a minute. But first I'm gonna teach this bastard not to mess in my yard. Then we'll talk about that fuckin' restraining order. We'll talk real nice. Yeah, real nice."

Clint had no strength for a fight. He was still recovering from the chemo and the drug-induced fatigue was still with him. And Abe looked to be as strong as an ox, and very angry. Besides that, Clint didn't want to fight with anyone. He wasn't a fighter. But here was a dangerous, drunk, and belligerent man in front of him and he had to do something. He had to protect himself and Wilma too.

He didn't know how to fight, but he did know one thing for sure and now he was going to use it. Abe was too formidable an assailant to try anything else on.

Without giving it any more than a moment's thought he kicked out as hard as he could right into Abe's groin. Abe doubled over and fell to the ground. Clint and Wilma ran inside the house. Clint called the police, begging them to hurry. Wilma stood in the middle of the living room, shaking and sobbing incoherently.

Abe, who wasn't feeling pain as he would have when sober, wasn't down for long. He started pounding on the door, then lunging against it.

The door had started to break apart just as a police officer drove up and saw what was happening. He ordered Abe to lie face down on the porch, but Abe wasn't going to let himself be arrested before he had dealt with Wilma and Clint. Not then; not when he was so close to getting his revenge. He leaped down the steps and charged the policeman, quickly pinning him to the ground and grabbing his pistol. He was aiming it at the officer's head when several shots rang out in quick succession.

Another squad car had pulled up in front of the house. The second policeman was just stopping his car when he saw his fellow officer about to be shot. He immediately pulled his own revolver and fired at the assailant without a moment's hesitation.

TWENTY-THREE

They were sitting next to each other on the back steps behind the Pharmacy. Clint had made lunch and brought it to her. They shared the salad and Wilma had a tuna sandwich with gobs of mayo while he enjoyed his tuna much drier. He could have had the Pharmacy's lunch counter staff prepare their meal, but he enjoyed making it himself at his temporary home.

The sunshine and warm breeze made it a perfect day for their mini-picnic. He had brought meals to her at work several times during the previous three weeks and knew she always enjoyed their time together during her lunch hour. She had finished eating and her lunch break was almost over. As the assistant manager she didn't have to punch a time card anymore and could take as long as she wanted, but she felt it important to set an example for the staff. She would return to work on time even though it meant leaving her love to do so, and even if he did own the company.

"Tomorrow on your day off will you look at a house with me?" he asked.

"A house? Whatever do you mean?"

"I've found a nice house that I might want to buy. But I want your opinion first."

"You're going to buy a house? Why didn't you tell me?"

"I wanted it to be a surprise. I was going to just buy one then surprise you. But after looking at several I've decided I really want your opinion on which one is best."

"Oh Clint, you're so special. Of course I'll look with you. I'd love to."

"Great! How's nine o'clock? You can come over and I'll fix us some breakfast then we can look at the house at ten?"

"That works. I'll see you then." After a lingering kiss, she arose and headed to the door and back to work.

"Bring Rocky too, for breakfast, if he's interested," he called after her.

Rocky and Teaser pulled up in front of Victor's house at eight the next morning, an hour early.

Clint opened the door before Rocky got to it and said, "I heard Teaser. I'm glad you came early. I can always use some help in the kitchen."

"Hi Dad," he said, having recently made a conscious decision to identify Clint as his father. "I've somewhere to go but I wanted to stop by first. Mom said you're going to buy a house?"

"Yep. Thinking about it, for sure. It's over on Yonkers Street, just across the field that's behind the Pharmacy. Will you have time to look at it this morning?"

"Nope. I wish I could. Will it have a garage for Teaser 2?"

"Absolutely. That's a firm requirement. Women like the inside of a house, but us guys want a nice big garage. The house I'm thinking about has a great garage, big enough for two cars and two motorcycles and more." He let his statement just hang there, waiting to see if Rocky picked up on it. But by that time Rocky was pouring some pancake mix onto the skillet and didn't catch the implied meaning.

"Speaking of motorcycles, I've been wondering about something," Rocky said. "Why did you want $182 for Teaser? Why not $200, or $100? Why $182?"

"When Meredith and I were first together I had an old motor scooter that I just loved. Well, I kept that old thing after we were married and I'd take it out for errands every chance I got. I wanted a real motorcycle but we couldn't afford it, so I just rode the scooter whenever I could. After a few years it barely ran anymore, then it quit altogether. So one year for my birthday Meredith surprised me big time with Teaser. She bought it with her own money for the down payment."

After wiping his damp eyes, Clint continued. "She paid every month, but then when she went away she still owed $182. So I finished the payments myself. Then when it came time for you to get the old girl it seemed appropriate to charge $182 for her. Somehow that seemed to be what Meredith would have wanted, too."

They were quiet for a minute or two, then Clint asked, "So where are you headed off to so early this morning?"

"I have a date with Sami. She's cooking me breakfast."

"So when do Wilma and I get to meet her? Or are you embarrassed about her meeting your parents?"

"Soon, Dad. Soon."

They sat at the table together while Rocky ate his pancake and some bacon that Clint had fried earlier. He only wanted a small meal, since his girlfriend would be cooking for him shortly.

Over the previous three weeks, since Abe had been shot by the policeman, Rocky and Clint had become very comfortable around each other. Rocky approved of his mom dating Clint, and was hoping that they would get together on a more substantial and permanent basis.

Clint had made it clear to Rocky that he was welcome to visit at any time of the day or night. They had also been enjoying motorcycling together, having taken several father and son rides through the countryside and up to the Blue Ridge Parkway. One time Wilma had also gone along, riding behind Clint, and they had all shared a very pleasant afternoon together that day.

Rocky was very busy with his part time job at the Pharmacy and his new girl friend. He and Sami had progressed physically to making out, but Sami had been very insistent that she wasn't going to go all the way with him at that point in their relationship. Nor would she tell him when, if ever, that might happen, and if that's all he wanted then he better just take a hike.

Meanwhile, just two days earlier they had agreed to an exclusive dating relationship, and both of them were getting used to this new type of commitment.

Sami's parents liked Rocky, and he spent as much time as he could at their house. Her brothers had pretty much gotten used to him and even played hoops with him in their driveway. Her mother was still elated that her tomboy daughter had been acting feminine, for the most part anyway, with her new boy friend. Sami and her mother had even gone clothes shopping together several times over the previous weeks so Sami could get some girl clothes.

On that morning, Sami was cooking for her man. She wanted to make him something special in commemoration of their new dating status. They hadn't seen each other since agreeing on the phone to be exclusive. She wasn't dating anyone else anyway, but the commitment felt wonderful. It felt like she imagined the other girls she knew must feel. Up until then she had always identified with how boys felt and feminine feelings were alien to her. But with Rocky she didn't want to be a tomboy. Somehow she felt it was time for her to be a girl.

Sami heard Teaser coming. She knew the motorcycle's exhaust sound and could hear Rocky coming from a block or more away. She got to the curb just as he pulled up. As soon as he dismounted she threw her arms around his neck and kissed him deeply, not caring if her parents or brothers saw her. He was her man now, and she wanted to kiss him right there in front of her house. He didn't mind. He didn't mind at all.

"So, do you like it?" he asked, trying to hide his feelings. He felt wonderful, anxious, and excited, all at the same time. He so wanted her to love the house, not just to like it. He had decided not to buy a house that she didn't love, but he wasn't going to let on how important this particular house was to him, or why, until she had chosen.

"Oh Clint, the outside looks wonderful. But let's see the inside before we get too carried away."

"Ok. The Realtor said she'd have it unlocked for us this morning. I saw the inside yesterday but I'm not saying what I think about it until you see it. Let's go."

Wilma was telling the truth when she said she loved the outside. She had always wanted a beautiful house with a broad front porch and an attached garage so she wouldn't be in the weather going to the car. And this house was obviously well cared for, not at all like the one she and Abe had lived in for so many years. And large, too. She had never dared hope for such a nice house before, since Abe's salary couldn't be stretched that far.

The house had an old southern style, but she knew it wasn't old at all. The previous residents had demolished the original house that had been on the lot and built the new home about five years before. It attracted the attention of all the local residents at the time because no one had ever heard of doing such a thing – demolishing a perfectly good house.

"Why is the house for sale?" she asked.

"I think the owners moved to Atlanta. They're pretty old and wanted to be near their children."

They had reached the front door and he found it to be unlocked just as the Realtor had promised. She already loved the outside, and just knew the inside would be wonderful too. And it was. It was about the size of the other large homes on the street that had hosted the towns more well-to-do residents for many years. The house had been well designed and she loved everything about it. It had two stories plus a basement, with three bedrooms, a den/office, large kitchen with modern appliances, dining room, living room, laundry room, and a couple of other rooms that she didn't know what they might be called.

"It's wonderful," she finally said, after racing through the house. "It's just wonderful. I love it. Really. Everything about it's wonderful. I'm sure you'll love it too."

"You haven't seen a couple of special areas yet. Follow me." He led her to the garage. "There's enough room for two cars and two motorcycles." He waited for her to realize what he meant.

"But you don't have two cars and two motorcycles."

"No, but what if it wasn't just me living here?" he asked, smiling broadly and nervously.

She stood there, trying to figure out just what he meant, and why he was smiling so sheepishly. Then it dawned on her and her heart leaped. She went to him, putting her hand on his chest, and barely squeaked out, "What do you mean, Clint?"

"It means I love you. I've loved you since that night we were together. That night that gave us Rocky. Even before that night, actually." He paused, then dropped to his knee. "Will you marry me, my darling Wilma?"

"That was great," Rocky said.

"Did you like the blueberry pancakes?" Sami asked.

"Oh yeah. It was all great. Thanks for doing that for me. That was a neat way to start our commitment to each other. Woman feeding man. I love it," he said, laughing the whole time so he could barely get the words out.

She jumped at him and tickled him mercilessly until he could barely catch his breath. When she finally stopped he had been pushed against the pantry door and she pressed up against him and kissed him lovingly. By the time she pulled away his body was shaking and he was breathing hard. "So, next time it'll be man feeding woman. And it had better be something you cook all by yourself, lover boy."

They cleaned up the kitchen and dishes together, talking and laughing the whole time. Then he asked, "Do you have anything planned for the rest of the morning? If not, there's two people I'd like you to meet."

"Ok, sure. Who?"

"My parents."

At the hospital the doctor and nurse recorded the time of death. Abe had never regained consciousness in the weeks since being shot by the policeman and his body had just succumbed.

Rocky found the house easily. Clint had told him which street, and his mother's car was parked in front of the house he thought it might be. He and Sami went to the open front door. When no one answered his knock, they went in and found his parents just in time to see Clint on his knee in front of Wilma. The moment Clint saw them he went to Rocky and asked if he could talk to him privately for a moment, and they went back to the living room.

"Rocky, my boy, I've just asked Wilma to marry me. I so hope that's all right with you. I want us all to be a family, if that's something you would like also. I had planned to talk to you first, but then the opportunity to ask her popped up so I took it. I'm pretty much on pins and needles right now."

"She hasn't answered you yet?"

"No. You came in just as I popped the question. Are you ok with her divorcing Abe and me asking for her hand?"

"Of course, Dad, I hoped you would. I want my mom and dad to be together. And Abe hurt her bad so I sure don't want them together ever again. But now we have to go find out what she says. Come on."

When they returned to the garage Sami and Wilma had already introduced themselves to each other. Clint apologized to the women for leaving so abruptly, and Rocky finished the introductions.

Clint went to Wilma, on his knee again, and asked her, "Will you marry me, Wilma?"

THE END

8856803R0

Made in the USA
Charleston, SC
20 July 2011